The Sounds At River's Edge

The Sounds At River's Edge: True stories of growing up on the Intracoastal Waterway
Copyright © 2022 by Bobbie J. McLaren

Published in the United States of America

ISBN   Paperback: 978-1-959165-00-2
ISBN   Hardback: 978-1-959165-20-0
ISBN   eBook: 978-1-959165-01-9

All rights reserved. No part of this publication may be reproduced, stored in a retrieval system or transmitted in any way by any means, electronic, mechanical, photocopy, recording or otherwise without the prior permission of the author except as provided by USA copyright law.

The opinions expressed by the author are not necessarily those of ReadersMagnet, LLC.

ReadersMagnet, LLC
10620 Treena Street, Suite 230 | San Diego, California, 92131 USA
1.619. 354. 2643 | www.readersmagnet.com

Book design copyright © 2022 by ReadersMagnet, LLC. All rights reserved.

Cover design by Ericka Obando
Interior design by Ched Celiz

The Sounds at
River's Edge

True stories *of* growing up
on the Intracoastal Waterway

By Bobbie J. McLaren

ReadersMagnet, LLC

Contents

A Leap of Faith 1
The Sound of Joy 7
A Father's Love 11
Broken Windows 15
Wounds and Memories 21
The Burning Bed 25
Fill'er Up 32
The Tooth Fairy 38
Runaway Train 44
The Demon Below 52
Who's been sleeping in My Bed? 59
Don't Leap This Frog 71
Keep Your Clothes On 80
No Monsters Allowed 86
The Sound of Terror 98
Time in a Bottle 107
Burnt Bridge 119
The Eye of the Storm 127
Summers on the Farm 140
Sailing Ships 149

In loving memory of Robert E. and Emma Jean McLaren. Parents, friends and teachers. They were someone to laugh with and sometimes cry, but always someone that knew more about me than I really understood.

Also, I would like to thank my sister Sherry for being there. For the friendship and encouragement that she has given. To Christine Walters for reading what I write and finding the errors, then correcting my mistakes. Christine and Sherry have been my rock when I was stumbling and gave me a place to be safe.

To Rhonda Dehart who gave a willing ear while I was creating and even encouraged me with laughter and stories of her own. She along with my church family at the Fort Payne Family Worship Center have lifted me when I felt weak and reminded me that family is bound by blood; blood that will always be thicker than water. The blood of Jesus.

Which brings all things to my Father, that is my life and my love. Thank the Lord for never letting me go and for loving me when I was most unlovely.

A Leap of Faith

Some of the greatest lessons I've learned, I learned while I was alone, on sailing ships to foreign lands or while hunting and exploring deep into the jungles. Maybe you did not have the sea at your back door as I did, and maybe your adventures are in places that I have not yet been. Still, I believe that if you were as I was, as a child, then you too know that adventures were as close as a thought and nearer than your next breath.

Remember with me now… Have you ever laid back in the grass to spot a cloud that looked like a dog, a duck, an elephant or even a submarine? Played connect the dots on a starry night? Found all the hidden objects in the *Highlights* magazine? What about putting playing cards on the spokes of your bicycle to make it sound like a motorcycle? If any of this sounds familiar, then come with me on a grand adventure of remembering.

As I have grown, I see the gross error that we as human beings have perpetrated upon our youth. I look back and I see how vivid my imagination was when I was a child. Oh how I could get lost in the pages of Nancy Drew or sail away to places like Treasure Island. Reading has become a lost art in many areas and I've even heard one youth say it was too close to homework. Instead of encouraging our young to expand their minds with the written word, we have trained them by using television and video games as baby sitters. In so doing, we have replaced our own importance to our children as their heroes. We have gotten so busy trying to make a life that we have forgotten how to live life.

I am not going to ask you to compare today's cartoons with yesterdays. There are enough people already on that soapbox and I have plenty of my own. In fact, I am rather fond of *Sponge Bob* and have used it many times as a stress reducer. There are many great animated shows that not only make you giggle but some even leave you with a lesson to learn. I am not the cartoon police and I am not going to tell you what you should or should not let your children watch on television. I will, however, tell you that as a child I had no reason to not believe what I saw on the screen. Oh brother...

For me to tell a story on page is so different from being able to see you face to face. You can't see my expressions or (so I've been told) the wild demonstration of me recounting my tale. So now it is your turn to imagine. Imagine me sharing my story with you with great wonder and excitement. Come now let me tell you a tale.

On Saturday mornings I would get up early, or at least it was hours before anyone else was up, and drag my favorite quilt into the living room. There I would settle down to watch cartoons, Looney Tunes to be exact. Daffy Duck was one of my favorite. I still smile just thinking of the many times Daffy would get his bill slapped off and the look of surprise on his face. Without a bill, his eyes appeared even larger than before. I never thought to rationalize how easy it was to knock it off or for him to simply pick it up and put it back on his face. All I knew was it brought large amounts of laughter and smiles. Laughter was my constant companion in those early morning hours as I lay on the floor with eyes wide in wonder.

There were back to back stories of Sylvester and Tweety, Porky Pig, Roadrunner, Bugs Bunny and Daffy. One particular episode had me completely in awe. It was about how Bugs Bunny was once again faced with the task to outwit Elmer Fudd. I watched in amazement as Bugs ran from Elmer just to find that he was in quite a dilemma. He had run until in front of him was a cliff with a very long drop. Behind him was Elmer with a gun. What to do! I had no doubt that Bugs was able to outsmart Elmer but this was a really big problem. Then reaching behind his back Bugs suddenly had an umbrella. The umbrella came open with a loud POP! As Bugs looked straight at me with a smile of satisfaction from knowing that once again he had outsmarted that bumbling wabbit hunter, he stepped off the edge of the cliff. Ever so gently he floated to the bottom safely away from Elmer.

WOW! I wanted to try that. I needed to try that but how? Remembering that Mom had recently gotten a new umbrella, I went to the hall closet where it was kept. It was a chocolate brown with gold tips and gold trim on the handle which was curled like and candy cane. Back then umbrellas were all long like walking sticks and this one was no exception. It was almost as long as I was tall so to sneak out of the house with it needed to happen now before anyone would be getting up to catch me. With umbrella in hand, and me still in my jammies, I went outside to the patio.

Now I needed to find a way up so that I would be able to come back down. Looking around the yard I spotted the perfect way to reach the roof of the house; a tree. As I climbed on top of the concrete picnic table I was able to reach one of the low limbs of one of the huge live oak trees that grew in the front yard surrounding the patio. This tree had a large limb that grew directly over to the top of our garage. The best part was that the limb began low then reached ever so gently upward toward the roof. The gradual slope was a great help to someone so small.

Once making my way to the limb I began inching across that branch. It was difficult but I straddled the limb like you would if you were riding a horse and moved forward in a squiggly fashion. Being small made it more of a challenge, but with fierce determination, I made it to the roof. Once in place I slowly walked to the edge replaying in my mind how that Bugs had floated so gently to the bottom of that steep cliff. With the umbrella (soon to be my parachute) in the open position I prepared for my descent. I looked carefully to see if anyone was visible in the house. I was still fairly certain no one else was awake. I did not want to get caught with mom's new umbrella. Certain that no one was around, I stepped off the roof.

I don't remember the time between that first step and the crouton bushes that now surrounded me. I can't explain how that the now crumpled and twisted umbrella had gotten under me, when moments before it was above me. I was so stunned that I didn't even realize that it was my Dad that was picking me up out of the hedge. When I finally looked into my Dad's face, I was torn somewhere between guilt for getting caught and the joy of being rescued. But oh… when I heard him laugh as he held me close to him, I knew that everything was going to be ok.

Mom never knew what had happen to her umbrella. Dad said that I had been through enough and that he would get her another. Sometimes we do crazy things just like jumping off the roof with an umbrella. When we see others doing something that looks like fun, something that will make us a part, something that will make us belong, we too step into danger. Danger, although we hate to admit it, has an exciting element all around it. We fear it and yet we embrace it. Then we discover that the fall is great and sudden. God is not going to stop us from disaster if we choose to go that way. He will not oppose our desire if we want to leap. Oh but when we see His mercy, His grace, His great love even in the mess that we have created, He will lift us up and care for our hurts.

> *I will extol You, o Lord, for You have lifted meup, And have not let my foes rejoice over me.*
> *Oh Lord my God, I cried out to You, and You healed me.*
> *o Lord, You brought my soul up from the grave;*
> *You have kept me alive, that I should not go down to the pit.*
> *Sing praise to the Lord, you saints of His, and give thanks at the remembrance of His holy name.*
> *For His anger is but for a moment, His favor is for life; Weeping may endure for a night, but joy comes in the morning.*
> *Psa. 30:1-5*

That is my Heavenly Father. Even when I have been foolish, He holds me close. There is nothing like the warmth and security of being in the arms of a loving father. The scratches and bruises I received in my fall are a vague memory. The thing that holds that story fresh in my mind is the trust of a child and the strength of my Dad. How would it have differed if Daddy weren't there to pick me up? Remember that child within you and let the Father embrace your situation today. There is no thing too big, too foolish or too hard for Him. Run as fast as you can into His arms and don't look back. The past will always be there, but it doesn't have to be your tomorrow. Just because a new umbrella replaced the broken one, did not change the fact that I was still bruised and scratched from my fall. I did however learn from the experience. I no longer leap from small buildings in a single bound.

The Sound of Joy

When do memories begin? At what age does the heart develop those fond recollections? This is not a subject that I am qualified to debate. All I know is that prior to my fourth year of living, I don't seem to have memory. Four was a big year for me. That was the year that my dad built our new home, the year that my sister broke my arm and the year that Pop died.

Although I was very young, I recall the times that we would go to Pop's house. It was the old homestead right next door and though that sounds really close, it really was not. The old house was built in the early 1900's before my dad and his twin sister was born in 1917. Built on the banks of the Intracoastal Waterway at one of the bends in the river it was not far from US 1. It was not a large house by today's standards but it was homey. There was a large fireplace in the center of the north wall of the living room. Above the mantle on two sides were large relief paintings. The colors were mixed with a concrete type mix and color added to create scenes of Florida. When the old house was tom down in the 1990's, my cousin saved the panels and was able to hang them in her home that was later built where the old homestead once stood.

Daddy would go regularly to Pop's house to cut corns off Pop's feet and each time he went, I went with him. The walk to Pop's was always an adventure. We would walk through an area completely undeveloped with all the natural beauty of an almost forgotten South Florida. It was a place were luscious mango trees grew in abundance surrounded by palm trees and palm bushes of every sort. Citrus was readily available at arms reach, as were avocados, guavas and numerous types of berries. A thick hedge of large Suriname cherry bushes enclosed Pop's front yard. There was a small but very hardy tree with the same kind of cherry growing outside the front door and I was never certain if the tree was an out of control bush or if the hedge was formed from trees that were well maintained.

There was a large gazebo with a wonderful concrete floor in front of the house, where years later I would spend many hours playing. Across the sidewalk to the west of the gazebo was a stone goldfish pond with a fountain in the middle. I never saw the fountain actually working, but I did enjoy the colorful goldfish.

Going to Pop's was one of the very best memories of my young life. Pop was a very big man especially to a very small child that thought that he was wonderful. I knew he would always be sitting just inside the living room door in his big chair with at least one foot on the ottoman. That was a time before recliners became common place, so to elevate your feet you would have to have an ottoman or a footstool.

Pop always made me feel as though he had been waiting all day just for me and that his day had been nothing until that very moment. Not just once but every time that we went, Dad would go before me, as I followed him to the front door, and he'd call in to let Pop know that we were there. As Dad walked inside, I was fast on his heels and Pop would ask, "Where's the boy?"

Little kids are so innocent, so impressionable and so trusting. I am not sure at what age that we gain the knowledge, or at least think that we have that we are too smart to fall for the same thing twice. But at that time in my life I would leap headlong into the same debate with Pop that would be prompted by that simple question, "Where's the boy?" I would quickly peek around Dad's legs and firmly state once again, "I'm not a boy, Pop!" His response never changed, never wavered, "Bobby is a boy's name so you must be a boy." With hands now firmly on my hips and a stance of defiance, I would challenge him again, "No Pop, I'm a girl with a girl's Bobbie." Then with a smile that would signal that the battle over and a laugh that filled the room his arms would reach out to draw me in, I eagerly ran to his embrace.

There was a safe place in that old man's arms. He would entice me into his world through challenge and each time I knew that the prize of the battle was not something material. No trophies, no awards of money or toys, just the warmth and comfort of a love that I knew was always there for me. Although he died before I turned five, I have memories of a man that could fill a room with laughter and melt the heart of a very small child. I don't remember his death, just the joys of the life that he shared with me even though the time was brief.

Proverbs 17:6, "Children's children are the crown of old men. And the glory of the children is their father."

Forty plus years later I still remember that old man and my heart smiles. Even as I write this, a smile has found its way to my face and warmth fills my body. If someone can make that much impact on a child in such a short amount of time does it not make you wonder what impressions are you leaving? How will we be remembered? I've heard it said that there are two types of people, those who light up a room when they enter and those that light the room when they leave.

> *Matthew 5:14 -16, "You are the light of the world. A city set upon a hill cannot be hidden. Nor do they light a lamp and put it under a basket, but on a lamp stand, and it gives light to all who are in the house. Let your light so shine before men that they may glorify your Father in Heaven."*

Let your light fill each room that you enter into as you pass through this life, just as Pop's laughter filled the house. You may never know whose life you have touched with warmth and comfort.

A Father's Love

The land where we lived was given to my Mom and Dad as a wedding present from Pop. It was a large tract of property that extended from EllisonWilson Road all the way to the river and then fifty feet passed the shoreline. That statement alone tells how much that the canal had broadened since my Dad's youth. Dad had built a picturesque house close to the road so that my Mom would be near activity, since not much happen in that very rural area. Activity meaning a car or truck passing the house, or maybe a delivery truck. Then there was the school bus that came by twice a day. That was the extent of the busy things she might see.

It was a cozy house with the front yard surrounded by a white picket fence. There was a bench made by placing wooden planks between two young oak trees so that as they grew the trunks would embrace the boards creating park like benches. Spanish moss hung from the limbs of the large live oak trees like jewels complimenting their stateliness. But the lure of the water called to my Mom and a new house was soon to be.

Except for his time in the Air Force during World War II and the Korean Conflict, my Dad worked construction all of his life. Building our new home was a labor of love. Many friends and co-workers helped him with their many talents and much needed labor, but it was Uncle Frank that seemed to be Dad's constant companion. And then there was me.

Since memory is limited, I don't recall when I was given my pedal driven jeep. It wasn't until the concrete floor was poured that I found my attachment to that four-wheeled wonder. Pedaling on the driveway was bumpy and challenging. Rocks and gravel would cause my forward movement to be slow and tedious. Large ruts would catch my tires and force my direction to change. I left the jeep parked for a while because it was too hard to fight the rocks and ruts. When the concrete was smoothed and set I discovered the joys of motoring.

The floor of the main living space in the new house was a wonderful platform on which to drive. Before any of the inner frameworks was erected, I had open space to zoom. As they began to connect the frames to the floor, I watched future walls now becoming an obstacle course to my once open roadway. I found it great fun to now drive from room to room as fast as was possible with sometimes missing the opening for the doors and slamming smack into the 2X4 studs. Even though there was 16 inches between the studs, I could not get my jeep through because of the 2 X 4 that was the base. I could not drive over them, and my mind didn't understand the jeep was too wide to go through them.

There was not a day that went by that I wasn't underfoot. As the men carried the assembled frames to their designated place, I drove, and drove, and drove. Several times they almost stumbled trying to avoid collision while carrying the walls. Everyday became more of a challenge as my open driving was diminishing. Before plastering the walls I could see from end to end inside the house. But now as I darted from room to room I never knew who or what would be in my way as I burst through the doorway.

The two largest rooms were the living room and the kitchen that were connected by one door. They sat side by side and because of their length I could reach incredible speed. Both rooms were the full width of the house and provoked in me the need to go as fast as was possible to enable the back end of my jeep to slide as I emerged from the doorway. The biggest problem I was faced with was the fact that I had to slow down to turn around to continue this mad race. Then one day I saw the workmen cutting another door into the wall where the living room connected with the dining area of the kitchen. This new doorway opened a whole new world to me and the race was now a non-stop loop.

You may wonder why I am sharing this story with you about a small child driving a pedal car. What is the point? Here is my reason: Years later, I found that there was only to be one door entering into the kitchen. In the original plans there wasn't a second doorway, but my Dad saw the struggle that I was having traveling from room to room. With great joy he changed the plans to accommodate his small child.

How great is the love of a father? How much more does your heavenly Father want good things for you?

> *Matthew 7:7-11, "Ask, and it shall be given you; seek, and you shall find; knock, and it shall be opened unto you: For everyone that asks receives; and he that seeks finds; and to him that knocks it shall be opened. Or what man is there of you, whom if his son ask bread, will he give him a stone? Or if he asks a fish,*

will give him a serpent? If you then, being evil, know how to give good gifts to your children, how much more shall your Father which is in heaven give good things to them that ask him?"

Some times it is the simple little things in life that we over look. When in reality, it is those simple things that have shaped our lives and molded our young spirit. Cherish those moments when someone has loved you for those are the memories to hold fast in your heart.

Broken Windows

I had this incredible thought that, what if… What if I could tell a story or series of stories in chronological order? I actually spent a great deal of time contemplating that very idea with absolutely no success. So what I have come up with is the idea that if I begin to write as I remember, or better, as the Holy Spirit brings to my memory, then I should be okay. With that out of the way let's travel on.

We had moved into the house where I made my great leap when I was four years old. I wasn't quite six when I climbed up into that oak tree. Just to give you some background history so you'll have a better understanding let me start with when, where, why (we're still not sure) *etc.* I was born in West Palm Beach, Florida in 1954. Yes, I am a baby boomer. But then so is my sister Sherry who preceded me in birth by four years. That is an important bit of knowledge as so much of my youth is some how intertwined with hers. We lived in a small community in the north part of Palm Beach County known as Juno. Growing up in south Florida was an adventure in itself.

Juno was a wonderful place to grow up. It was quiet, wooded and everyone knew each other. We never locked our doors and when I was very young, I could leave the house and be gone for hours and my parents didn't worry because all the neighbors watched out for each other's children. I know that it sounds a lot like "Walden's Mountain" but being only three feet above sea level, a mountain it definitely was not.

My Dad and some of his friends built the house where I grew up. The Intracoastal Waterway was the property line for our backyard. We called it the "canal". A name passed down from my Dad's family that homesteaded there in the early 1900's. At that time, the river was only 30 feet wide behind my grandpa's home. As time passed from my grandfather's life to mine, the canal broadened and deepened by repeated dredging. It now is a very wide and very deep river that has become a freeway for boats. But I am getting ahead of myself. The canal was usually quiet and not much traveled during my youth. There were a few pleasure boats, the occasional tug boat and barge and then there was the sightseeing boat. Each time it went by in the night it would blow its horn and we would flick our lights at the back of the house.

So much of my life developed by that waterway and the surrounding woods, it developed in me a love for the water, which I still love. The sound of the waves gently lapping against the shore, the smell of the salt in the air. These are things that trigger memories. Memories of wonder and excitement. Come with me now on a journey to a quieter, milder time of innocence. Innocence was not something that I was often associated.

My grandfather known as "Pop" owned a large amount of land in Juno. That is how that my parents came to build next door to the 'old home place'. My Dad was born in that old house. He and his twin sister were the first in their family born in the United States, and the last of ten children. When my Dad came home after World War II with a bride, Pop gave them property as a wedding present. There was family property all around us, which was great (unless you were into mischief).

Aunt Clara, one of Dad's sisters, had rental houses nearby. One of the houses was on the corner of EllisonWilson and McLaren Road. This house was at one time the bridgetenders house. When the drawbridge was destroyed in the 1949 hurricane, the county decided to not rebuild the bridge. The bridgetenders house was then moved to that corner lot. There was a circular driveway in front of the house that connected from one road to the other. In front of the driveway were hedges and plants that attracted many birds and squirrels. This was a place that I liked to hide, a place that eventually would lead me into trouble.

I was not allowed to have a BB gun when I was young. I guess my parent's thought that I might shoot my eye (or better still) my sisters eye out. I was allowed however, to have a sling shot. Big mistake! I really liked shooting things with my slingshot. One of my best friends named Al, was given all kinds of guns and he gave me some BB's. I decided to try doing some target practice with the BB's at Aunt Clara's comer house. As I lay in the bushes so no one could see me, I aimed at some of the cherries on the surrounding trees. BB 's were smaller than what I was used to using. It was taking some real concentration to get that tiny ball to go where I was aiming. And then it happen... PING!

I heard a sound that was not familiar to my ears. It was a kind of ping. Looking around I saw a very small hole in the beautiful picture window on the front of the house. Since no one was home, I crept closer to see if that could have been the source of the sound. What I found was one of the most amazing things I had ever seen. There was indeed a small hole in the glass about the size of the BB, but on the inside it appeared to have a much larger piece of the window missing. A piece about the size of a dime was on the inside of the little hole.

Quickly I returned to my place of safety in the hedge. I wasn't sure that I had done this but I had to know. So with caution, so that I wouldn't get caught, I lay down on the ground and took aim. PING! Oh yeah, that was the sound. I ran over to the window and was again fascinated by the way that there was only a small hole on one side, yet a much larger hole on the other side. I was hooked. I now emptied my pocket of BB's into the window. Wow! By the time I was done, there were probably fifty holes in that picture window. With no BB's left, I went home.

Later that night after my Dad got home, he came and asked me if I knew anything about someone shooting the picture window at Aunt Clara's with a **BB** gun. I thought for a minute before answering him and then told him that I did not know anything about anyone shooting that window with a BB gun. He stood looking at me with that "I know you know something" look on his face and then asked me one more time, "Bobbie, do you know anything about someone shooting a **BB** gun near your Aunt Clara's house that might have accidentally hit her window?" Standing firm with my first answer, especially since it really wasn't a lie. I again stated that I knew nothing about anyone using a **BB** gun near her house. With that answer, he looked at me with a smile and stood up to go inside. He reached down and mussed my hair before walking away.

My Dad was a lot smarter then I liked. He came to me the next night and asked me a different question. He sat down on the edge of the front porch with me and looking straight ahead he asked, "Do you know anything about someone hitting the window at Aunt Clara's with BB's?" This was a trap. He still was not looking at me while I sat next to him trying to come up with something that would get me out of this dilemma. I shuffled my feet, squirmed around on my bottom and played with the small twigs at my feet. We sat there for what seemed an eternity. Ok, it was probably only two or three minutes, but when your about to get caught, those minutes just go on, and on, and on.

I finally asked, "What's gonna happen to the person that did it?" That question was met with silence. Then, just when I thought maybe he decided that it really wasn't a big deal, he looked straight at me and said, "The person that did it, is going to have to pay for the window." I looked back at him and began to spill my guts. I explained how that it was just an accident. I told him how that I was aiming at a cherry and missed. He asked me how fifty holes could be accidental. He could understand one hole, not fifty. It was too late to retreat. I explained how that I was amazed by the way that there was such a tiny hole on one side yet a big hole on the other. I couldn't stop until I had used all the BB's I had.

Needless to say, I paid for that window for a very long time out of my allowance (or so I thought). In reality, Dad paid for my mischief. When my allowance was only a quarter a week, I would have been paying for years. But because of the love of a parent, who knew that as children we would make mistakes, He paid the price for me. I did have to apologize to Aunt Clara and promise to not shoot anymore windows with anything. I really thought I was clever about telling dad that I didn't know about the shooting with a BB gun. He didn't ask me about a slingshot. Unfortunately I tried carrying that type of thought life into my adult life and even tried using it with God. But, no matter how old you are, you will always be Gods' child and subject to approval. In Proverbs 3:1-8, it says,

> *"My son, forget not my law; but let thine heart keep my commandments: For length of days, and long life, and peace, shall they add to thee.*
> *Let not mercy and truth forsake thee: bind them about thy neck; Write them upon the table of thine heart; So shalt thou find favour and good understanding in the sight of God and man.*
> *Trust in the Lord with all thine heart; and lean not to thine own understanding.*
> *In all thy ways acknowledge him, and he shall direct thy paths. Be not wise in thine own eyes: fear the Lord, and depart from evil. It shall be health to thy navel, and marrow to thy bones.*

Learning to not be what I thought was wise has been a challenge. Sometimes it has caused much pain and sorrow. But understanding that you can't play word games with God or with man with success has set me free. Often the price seems high for the errors we have made, but no price will ever match the one paid at the cross. All the clever ways we try to fool God serve only to trap us in a web of deceit that the destroyer has had in place since the garden. We hide in the bushes hoping He'll not see our mistakes. It is time to come out and stand bare before the Father. For He knows all. Broken windows or shattered dreams turn them all over to Him and let the healing begin.

Wounds and Memories

As I earlier stated, my sister Sherry had quite a bit to do with my tender years of growing. Separated by four years is not that much but just enough to sometimes create chaos. One of my dad's brothers, Uncle Jim lived a couple of houses away with his wife, Aunt Lucille and their two daughters Betty and Shirley. Betty was much older than I was, or so it seemed when I was a small child, and Shirley was about the same age as Sherry. Sherry and Shirley spent a great deal of time playing together. Many times when Sherry would go over to their house, I went too. I was not always welcomed or wanted.

Betty and Shirley had the most awesome toys. If there was a popular toy or doll of the time, they had it. I was always excited about going to their house with Sherry for two reasons. One, there weren't very many other kids around for me to play with and two, I was going to get to play with some of their toys. I was even willing to tolerate the torture that I was guaranteed if I followed Sherry. It wasn't like they tied me to an ant pile, although they probably would have like to. And they never tied me to a tree like they did Sherry, but that's a different story (which I had no part of). The worst thing they would do was to lock me in a closet with whatever toys that they weren't playing with and with toys that they knew would keep me quiet.

That may sound harsh but when you recall that they had all the neatest games, toys and Barbie's, even the throw offs were really a lot of fun. I grew to enjoy the time I spent in that cubicle and even found a sense of security in knowing that I was safe. As long as I could hear the sounds of laughter and activity nearby, I knew that I was not alone.

Behind Uncle Jim's house was a large dock that extended out over the river where he worked on all types of tugboats, barges and yachts. The dock was in a "L" shape with the "L" end of it facing north. It was able to accommodate more vessels with that design. Companies from all over south Florida would bring their large equipment to him for repairs. The yard was usually filled with bulldozers, cranes and other earthmovers. His welding talents only matched his mechanical abilities. If there were parts needed that he could not find, he would create the needed part.

Uncle Jim was a tall lanky man, especially when you are a small child, but even as I grew, he was still a man of great stature. Well over six feet tall and slim like a pencil; he would tower over Aunt Lucille who stood just at five feet tall. As contrasts would go, you had a man of Scottish-Irish decent who was very laid back and usually even-tempered coupled with a fiery hot-tempered American Indian of the Miami tribe.

When Aunt Lucille was mad it would not have been wrong to label it a "warpath". Yet, as different as they were, they loved one another and their children deeply, and I loved them.

One day the two girls, Sherry and Shirley, decided to take the small wooden boat that was tied at the dock for a ride. Can you guess who followed? Yeah, that would have been me. The boat called a dinghy was tied in the shallows and with the tide out, you had to jump down quite a way to get into the boat. Sherry and Shirley had a much easier time getting into the boat since they were taller. I did not have such an easy time. They had run on ahead and they were both in the stern of the boat as I came near. Just as I was to jump down into the dinghy, they pushed it away from the dock. I landed in the very tip of the bow on top of an old Maxwell House coffee can that was kept in the boat for bailing water. Coffee cans at that time were only three to four inches tall and made of metal. The rim of that can sunk into my right heel as deep as my heel bone would allow.

I remember turning and looking at Sherry and Shirley just before climbing back up onto the dock. I was never sure what they thought only that I was not going to let them see me cry. I do however, remember them calling out to me that it was my fault since I shouldn't have followed them. And I remember hollering back to them, "You'll be sorry!"

I ran/hopped to the house where I found Aunt Lucille. There I shed a crop of tears as she immediately went to work on my wound. She did not console me with immediate revenge on those two monsters. She just focused on the job at hand of cleaning the gaping slit that ran from one side of my foot to the other. She cleaned, covered and wrapped my foot with great care and when she finished with the medical treatment she treated me with a cold drink and a comfortable chair. A place where I could sit with my foot up and watch something on television. Then she left for the dock.

I never got to see the interaction between her and my tormentors, but I did see the "we will get you later" looks that they gave me as they passed through the room. I went every day for the next two weeks for Aunt Lucille to change the dressing over the wound. Every day during that time, I was able to play with the toys of my choice since there was no competition. I think that Sherry was grounded from going over to Shirley's for a while because I did not see her over there for some time. Today, I would have been taken to the hospital for stitches because of the depth of the cut, but all I bear on my body is a scar of a well-tended accident.

Proverbs 10:7, "The memory of the just is blessed..."KJV
"We all have happy memories of good men gone to their reward..." Living Bible.

Some may say that I don't see the clearly all the elements that were involved in each incident. That is not really the most important thing to me. What I choose to see is the love and concern that was shown to me when I was growing up. There will always be challenges if there are other people. We don't live alone, we don't develop alone. The things that happen between my sister and me were normal child hood events based on the things that were surrounding us. Not every one grew up around the water. Not everyone lives in Florida. And not everyone has a friend in their sister as I do today.

The Burning Bed

Sometimes looking back it did seem like they were simpler times and yet there were times of great complexities. Today we would no more leave a child alone when they are six or seven years old than you would run naked through the streets. I say alone, although I was not really since my sister Sherry was somewhere nearby. Remembering that she is four years older than me should give comfort that I was well taken care of when mom and daddy weren't home. But then I guess that would depend on how you would perceive the situation. During the week, dad worked construction while Mom was a part time banquet waitress at the George Washington Hotel in West Palm Beach. There really was not a lot of time for us to be left on our own, just enough time to get into trouble. Such was this time...

Many of the homes in the surrounding area were homes that were filled with family. My Mom's youngest sister, Aunt Dolores with her husband, Uncle Freeland and their three (later to be four) boys lived next door off and on during my youth. I recall playing and fighting with all three boys. Sometimes it was one at a time, while other times I took on all three. Freeland, Jr., called Butch was a year older than I was, while Jeffrey was thirty-one days younger. Then there was Greg. Greg was not quite three years younger than I was but due to his age he was easier to bully around and was usually willing to play whatever game that I wanted to play. Sometimes our playtime turned into trouble. This is a story of one such event.

This day Mom and Daddy were both at work and I was in the tender care of Sherry. That meant that I needed to play either in the house so that she wouldn't have to hunt me down, or play wherever she was. If she ever had to look for me or if I "accidentally" hid in a place where she couldn't find me, there were to be dire consequences. So this day I chose to play indoors.

Greg had come over and we had played with my matchbox cars and trucks until boredom set in. There were no cartoons on television and since that was a time (believe or not) before VCR's and home videos, we began to look for something else to play. How far does a child have to look before finding something that they should not be involved in? How close is trouble to your children in your home, not far at all. My trouble began with one of my dad's favorite collections.

From as far as my memory allows my Dad collected old lighters. He had quite an assortment that varied both in size and style. Most of the lighters were of the type made for keeping on top of a table either next to the sometimes-matching ashtray or pipe stand. There were small plain lighters and then there were large ornate ones, to use them you would need to use both hands, even as an adult. The thing that I had always fascinated me was the awesome spark that you would see when pushing down the lever on the top. When boredom tried to overtake us, the call of those wondrous trinkets began to beckon.

I knew that I would be in a heap of trouble if I were caught with Dad's lighters so off to a dark closet with our treasures. Greg was so trusting and such fun when we were young. I, too, saw no danger in the desire to play with those forbidden flame makers since there wasn't any lighter fluid in any of them. We each had two lighters to play with in the darkness, but finding the right spot was quite a challenge. Why I chose to go to my Mom's closet I will never know, unless it was because I knew it was the farthest spot from where Sherry would be and the least likely for her to look for us. But Mom's closet was packed full of clothes, shoes and stuff. Lots and lots of stuff, too much clutter for us to be able to be thrilled with the spark from our own lighter so we emerged to find a better dark place.

Then I saw it. .. Mom and Daddy's bed! Covered with this wonderful white chenille bedspread that hung all the way to the floor I saw another great spot of darkness. Greg saw where I was headed and followed with lighters in hand. We crawled under the bed and began flipping the lighters open. The flints were still intact and made such a splendid flash each time we mashed the buttons. Now the only problem was that we were too close to each other to really enjoy our own individual light. The solution to that problem was simple; I would turn and face the other direction while Greg stayed where he was. This worked out very well until…

Flicking the lighters as fast as possible so that I could create a lightning effect, I was completely absorbed with my own display. Greg began tugging at my leg in a very annoying way. I remember telling him to leave me alone and play with his own lighters. He persisted in pulling on me until I finally turned to see what he wanted. When I turned, I saw a light that was not coming from his lighter. This light was more constant than flashing and this light was full of heat. The sparks from the lighter had somehow caught on the fringe of that chenille bedspread and was now a full flame. When you are seven and your accomplice only four or five years old there isn't a lot of experience or knowledge of what do you do in this situation. So my only recourse was to find Sherry.

As we ran from the bedroom I sent Greg out the back door and told him to go home. As he fled from the rear of the house I ran to the front where I knew I would find my sister. Storming out the front door and into the garage I almost ran over her in my haste to find her. Grabbing her left arm, I began to scream and pull at her. In my panic I don't think she really understood what I was trying to communicate to her and in frustration she pushed me away. Fear gripped my being as I again pulled at her while speaking so fast she would have needed an interpreter to understand my babbling. Finally in desperation I yanked at her until she almost fell on top of me while I pulled her to the front porch where smoke was already billowing out the bedroom window. There was a time of absolute silence and astonishment while we both stood with eyes gaped wide open and fixed on that eerie sight.

Sherry ran like the wind across the yard to Aunt Lucille's house with me in tow. It becomes a blur as to what happen next with everything moving so swiftly. I knew that Aunt Lucille had called the fire department before running over to our house with us. I remember the dreadful black smoke that began to billow from the window after she pushed the garden hose through the window into the bedroom and then rushed into the house. I was told the dark smoke was created when she began dousing the bed in water.

I recall standing with Sherry on the front porch watching in terror while not knowing what was happening inside the room.

Then I heard the sound of the siren as the fire truck approached. It was a sound that seemed to give me comfort in knowing that real help was on the way, yet it was Aunt Lucille that saved the day, even though the Fire Department was only a couple blocks away. By the time the firemen made their way into the bedroom, Aunt Lucille had successfully extinguished the flames. They served to verify that all was safe and then helped to remove the smoldering mattress.

With the arrival of the firemen, I felt somewhat at ease knowing that everything was going to be all right. Then the nearness of the fire truck began to call out to me and I immediately responded. There were so many gauges, dials and levers on the vehicle. The incredible way that the hoses were folded and rolled in the different places was awe-inspiring. I stood mesmerized by the shine of the silver sides and red body of this chariot of hope until suddenly I heard a sound coming down the driveway, it was Dad's panel truck. There were so many emotions surging through my mind and body at that moment that I don't even have a way to describe it.

I never moved as Dad parked his truck or even when he started to get out of it. I stood frozen in space and time as I watched him walk toward me, it seemed like an eternity. As he reached my side, he looked at the fire truck and then at the house and then at me. I don't ever recall my Dad in a panic, although I was at that moment. He looked again at the fire truck and began to ask me what was going on? Fear grabbed me like a magnet and my mind began to swim looking for a lifeline that would save me from drowning. But I knew I was going down.

Speaking as quickly as possible and hoping that if I was completely honest, with the exclusion of telling him that Greg had been there also, I recapped the events. I don't remember how long it was between the time that he went into the house to speak with the firemen and assess the damage and the time before returning to me. I do remember him calling to me and upon my arrival, him pulling his belt off in one quick movement. That sound is forever etched in my memory.

What happen next would by today's standards been deemed child abuse, but trust me it was not. He left an impression on both my back side and my understanding that I was to never play with any type of fire, lighters or anything of that nature without parental supervision. Then the worst of the entire event took place: he sat down next to me and calmly explained that if Aunt Lucille had not been able to extinguish the fire as she did, then there was a chance that the entire house could have be consumed. His voice was even and smooth as he expounded on how that I could have burnt down the home that he and Mom had worked so hard to provide for us. Sometimes I look back and honestly believe that I would have preferred for him to spank me again then for him to speak to me with a heart full of hurt.

> Hebrews 12:6-9, *"For whom the Lord loveth he chasteneth, and scourgeth every son whom he receiveth. If ye endure chastening, God dealeth with you as with sons; for what son is he whom the father chastenth not? But if ye be without chastisement, whereof all are partakers, then are ye bastards, and not sons.*

Furthermore we have had father of our flesh which corrected us, and we gave them reverence; shall we not much rather be in subjec tion unto the Father of spirits, and live?"

How great is a father's love? The Bible teaches us that God only corrects those that are His. My Dad did not punish me because of the loss of a physical possession, but because of the love he had for me, his child. He always taught me that "things" can be replaced but people can't. He later explained how fire can get so quickly out of control it will devastate everything in its path. I will never forget his look of concern when he said to me, "What if you hadn't been able to get out from under the bed?" You can't conceal true love and concern, and in that moment I briefly forgot the pain I suffered from his belt and could only feel the warmth of a father that truly loved me.

Fill'er Up

As time goes on you will see that not all my adventures with Sherry were devastately painful for me. Sometimes we actually played well together. Not that that happened often, yet it did occur at times. One such event I would like to share with you now. It occurred on a hot summer day while Sherry was out of school for the summer. I would have also been out for the summer if I had been able to stay in kindergarten. But due to an out of control fear, I would cry every day and the teacher would have to go and get Sherry out of her classroom to come and calm me down. How ironic it is that the person that can sometimes be your biggest pain at home can also be your greatest comfort elsewhere.

From the farthest reaches of my memory I recall a quilt that was given to me as a baby (or so I've been told) by Mrs. Wilson. That quilt was my security blanket at home. I could not sleep without it and when we traveled, it was my constant companion, even in the car. The school officials would not let me carry my quilt with me to class so I had to face that foreign environment all alone. That is when I discovered that the person that I thought was my tormenter had really become my security.

With summer pounding around us with waves of heat we began looking for reasons to play in the water. Sherry wanted to go swimming but Shirley wasn't home and I did not know how to swim. Dad had told us that we could not go swimming alone and even though Mom was home, she too could not swim and was deathly afraid of the water. If you can't swim in the river and we had no pool (dad said we didn't need one because we had a huge swimming pool in the back yard called "the canal"), we decided it was time to play with the hose.

We did not have city water at that time with our home being so far in the county and no city claiming us, so the water that we used was straight out of the ground; Well water. Unlike the wells that are dug in the mountains of North Alabama where you have to dig sometimes over a hundred feet down before hitting an underground river, the water table in Florida was only 20 feet down to the source of our well. Our home was only three feet above sea level and we were surrounded by water on all sides, which made water readily available. Just as a side note, whenever there were hurricanes we would become very aware of that fact that water surrounded us, for to leave our home we had to cross over bridges to reach the mainland. So to say that we were wrapped around by water would not be an exaggeration.

The faucet was on the side of the garage right next to the walkway that I had leaped over when I made my great flight from the roof. There was a green garden hose that was always connected to the faucet. This was the place that we decided to find relief from our suffering. When a hose has been lying for awhile in the sun, the water that was inside it tends to be a bit hot. I can't say that Sherry knew for sure what she was doing when she turned the handle on that spigot, but all that hot water came spraying out all over me. I remember screaming until, suddenly there was a sudden burst of relief as the cool water followed and covered my being.

Ahhh, what a wonderful sensation to feel the heat beginning to ease in your body. Just as I thought that I had found heaven, Sherry turned the hose on herself. I was a very selfish child at times and immediately a fight began. As we battled over the hose we were both getting drenched with that cool water as it was being pulled from side to side. I think that the fight was more fun than we would want to admit with water spraying in every direction as we strived for dominance. The times that Sherry had the hose she would hold her thumb over the end to create a stronger spray and chase me around, then a brief struggle and I would be chasing her.

This went on for a while until we were sufficiently cooled down and now looking for something else to play. Not wanting to give up our water supply yet, we tried to find something that might be fun and could involve our friend, the hose. Sherry turned the water off while we looked around for something else to do. Then she found it, we would play gas station. Mom and Daddy's car, a 1959 black Buick Electra was parked inside our two-car garage. Sherry was going to be the station attendant and I was going to be her assistant. The problem was that I wasn't strong enough to turn the handle on the faucet so Sherry had to turn it just enough to stop the flow of water but not tight enough to where I could not turn it on.

The plan was devised and now I stood at my station. Sherry pulled the hose over to the car and I could hear her speaking to the pretend occupant of the car. "Hi, can I help you? You want me to fill'er up? One moment while I turn on the pump". That was my cue, and as quick as lightning I reached to the tap and turned that faucet on. Standing like a soldier on a mission I waited for my signal to stop the dispensing of that fuel. Then I heard Sherry yell that the tank was overflowing. As fast as my little fingers could go I turned that knob until the water shut completely off. By the time I had it turned off, Sherry had come around the corner with the end of the hose in hand and a look of frustration. I wasn't fast enough to play gas station with her anymore so this game was over. After turning the handle so that it was really tight and no sign of water oozing from the end of the hose, Sherry went off to play something and somewhere else than where I would be. I am not certain as to the length of time that our service station adventure had ended when Dad arrived home. I remember the feeling of safety when I saw his old green 1949 Ford panel truck coming down the driveway. Sitting on the picnic table on our patio at the front of the house, I waited for Daddy to get out of his truck and come around the corner of the garage. When he stepped around where he saw me sitting he walked over with a smile and commented on my washed look. I was so eager to share my day with him that I couldn't wait any longer.

Leaping down from the table and running to him I began to unveil the wonders of the day. How he ever understood what I said will always be a mystery. I would speak so fast that it would appear that you would need an interpreter just to get the meaning. My speech has slowed considerably since moving to Alabama but that was not the case at that time. Looking at me with a look of bewilderment, he said for me to slow down and say that last sentence again. Taking a deep breath I again recapped the highlights of the day. Putting his hand gently on my shoulder he asked what do you mean about the car?

What joy to tell my Dad how that he wouldn't have to go to the gas station for a while since we filled the tank for him. This brought on a look that I still am not sure what it meant. I walked with Dad over to the garage and to the rear end of the Buick, as he gazed at the gas tank door that actually was the license plate. Looking at me again he asked me what we filled the car with. Excitement was about to knock me down as I proudly told him of our gas station adventure. The look on his face went from a look of bewilderment to a look of pain; a look as if someone had punched him in the stomach type pain. The next few minutes were spent with me giving him the full details as to how the entire event came to be. From the hot water bath to the moment that Sherry became bored with the game. He never said a whole lot after listening to my full recollection of a day well spent. He told me to go inside and get cleaned up for dinner. As I started for the front door he stopped me long enough to have me carry his old metal lunch box to the kitchen I'm not sure how long he stayed outside after I went in to clean up, but I know that we waited dinner until he finished whatever it was that he was working on outside. I later found that the job he was doing involved draining the gas tank on Mom's car. When he came in for supper and sat at the head of the table, he blessed our food and our home. The conversation at dinner was all about not ever filling the tank on the car, the truck or the lawn mower with water. He did not go into detail but he did make a strong argument as to why we won't do that again.

Proverbs 4:1-6, Hear, my children the instruction of a father, and give attention to know understanding: For I give you good *doctrine: Do not forsake my law. When I was my fathers son (daughter*), tender and the only one in the sight of my mother, He also taught me, and said to me: Let your heart retain my words; keep my commands, and live. Get wisdom! Get understanding! Do not forget, nor turn away from the words of my mouth. Do not forsake her, and she will preserve you; love her, and she will keep you."*

Most of the correction that was given to us from dad was done with great mercy and controlled tones. Thinking back it makes me wonder what type of child my Dad had been for him to take so many crazy things that we would do in such stride. He seemed to understand our many foolish antics. May it be that all of us never forget the childish things that we have done while growing up. I pray that each of you not only remember, but allow compassion and mercy to be your brand of punishment with your children. Pass wisdom and love to your heirs, as it will be their greatest inheritance.

The Tooth Fairy

As small children we hear of many fables and myths. Questions fill our young minds about Santa Claus, the Easter Bunny, and the boogie man and of course the tooth fairy. Are they real? Do they exist? Where do they live? So many questions go unanswered and when you have adults around you that skirt the issues not wanting to destroy the hopes of Christmas or the wonders of Easter, the truth is often lost. But the boogie man illusions need to be crushed along with the fears that his very name evoked. The fictitious boogie man is not real, does not exist and lives no where but in the minds of those who allow fear to be their companion. And shame on all of you that have used him as leverage to control your children. Leaving that behind, let's move ahead to the only one that I listed above that seems to have a secretive life, the tooth fairy. I had heard stories of how you would place your latest loss under your pillow and during the night while you slept, the tooth fairy would come and exchange money for your tooth. First of all, I am so glad that that was not the case in my life. With all the fears I had of things in the night, I would have totally freaked out if I were awakened to find a winged stranger groping under my pillow for my lost treasure while I slept. We are not talking about a winged angel but a mythical fairy that people talked about, yet no one seemed to know exactly where this creature came from. Santa Claus not only had a home but he had an entire community of elves and a wife. We knew what he wore and the types of food that he liked especially the type of cookies that were needed to be left out for him on his long journey.

The Easter Bunny lived in the woods and spent all year gathering eggs to color and created chocolate images of himself to share on his special day. There were even books written about his adventures and tales with many of his friends. You knew it had to be true if it's in print. So who was this tooth fairy? Where did this idea form and why did so many people further the tale? So many questions went unanswered about that fairy of flight that had no home, no written history and again where did he or she put all those teeth? How many children besides me were plagued with unrealistic fears and really did not look forward to a nighttime encounter?

When my first tooth began to loosen I began to think of the creature that was to come to my house to gather my first casualty. As a six-year- old I found that praying to God would fill me with hope and settle some of the fears that tried to spring up in my mind. I can't say that I fully understood the power of prayer or that there was a God that loved me and cared about every tooth and every hair on my being, but I did know that He was bigger than anything that would try to come and harm me.

As the first tooth began to wiggle I found myself showing everyone and telling them of my approaching dilemma. On one of the many visits I made to Aunt Lucille's house, this was one of those deliberate journeys filled with purpose. That purpose was to show

Aunt Lucille my soon coming loss and to hear her ideas of who and what this magical visiting fairy was all about. I am not sure why I trusted so much of what she would tell me or why I so quickly believed her explanation of things that I did not understand. All I do know is that she seemed so sure about what she spoke of and in her calm assurance I found a gentle peace.

Walking into the front of the house you entered into a type of Florida room or enclosed porch that lead into the living room. Aunt Lucille was a collector of antiques and her home was full of very old, some very expensive pieces of furniture. There were chairs and hutches that were beautifully carved and ornate, made of hand crafted woods and polished to show every detail. Looking back it seems strange that she allowed us to sit and play on the furniture, as long as it was not roughhousing, with it being so valuable.

Still, my memories of her, are of a mother that cared more about her family than she did the pieces she collected. There was one old Grandfather clock that stood like a silent sentry in the small hall that divided two of the bedrooms. Of all the furniture in the living room that clock and Uncle Jim's chair were the only two pieces that were never moved when other pieces were rearranged.

Entering the living room I would look first, then yell if necessary to let Aunt Lucille know I had arrived. She always made me feel that she was pleased I had come for a visit, even if Shirley or Sherry would groan if they were anywhere nearby when I came through the doorway.

But I had a mission as I entered her house that day with my wobbly tooth. My mission was to show her my tooth and find out everything that she knew of that "Tooth Fairy". I was certain that if anyone knew the truth about the tooth fairy it would be Aunt Lucille. She was so patient with me as I explained my situation to her. She had a way of looking at you that made you think that what you were saying was the most important thing in the world to her. At the end of my long discourse, she sat for a long moment and then told me that there was a way to avoid a tooth fairy encounter.

What! Could it be true, could it be possible to avoid having that stranger enter my room in the middle of the night? Was there really a way to keep the creature's hand out from under my pillow while I slept? This was too exciting to believe but I had to know what could be done to prevent it. She began to explain that if I were to let her pull my tooth when it was ready to come out that she would give me fifty cents for my tooth and then the tooth fairy would have no reason to come to my house. With that information in mind I went to her house everyday for the next two weeks for her to check my tooth. Then the day finally arrived that she said my tooth was at the point of coming out.

I was fine with the thought of her pulling my tooth until that day actually arrived. Now I was faced with the idea of her yanking my tooth, a tooth that had been with me forever, or so it seemed, out of my head while blood pumped out of my gums. Okay that may be a little far fetched with the details but you have to remember I was only six and I had a very vivid imagination. She must have sensed the fear or maybe she saw it etched on my face as she came close to check one more time. As she gazed into my mouth she began to tell me of a method that was almost pain free and would happen so fast that it would fool my gums into believing that my tooth was still there. This was definitely too good to be true. As I listened to her explain the "sewing thread method" I could feel my body relaxing a wee bit. Not enough to just jump into doing it but well on my way to the point of thinking I could stand this possible method.

The "sewing thread method" was simple; it was the thread from one of her spools tied ever so gently around the base of my loose tooth. Then she began the most amazing adventure a person can have inside of one room. She would carefully unroll the thread from the spool and leaving plenty of slack from the spool to my tooth, she began a journey around the room. She ran thread around a doorknob, then through the arm of a chair, up over the grandfather clock. From the clock, the spool was taken under the sofa and around one leg before going under the coffee table. By the time she made her way around the room, pass the fireplace and over toward the open secretary, I was enthralled by the weaving of the thread that was attached to my tooth.

Now placing the spool down on the arm of Uncle Jim's chair, she came over to check one last time on my tooth. As she reached into my mouth to feel the readiness of my tooth, I gazed around the room following the trail of the thread. Looking away, waiting for her to go back to the spool to pull my tooth free I was stunned to suddenly see my tooth in between her fingers. I would like to say that I only fell for this one time but two more teeth would be pulled in like manner before I was quick enough to not fall for the same thing. All three times I was so interested in the trail that she made with the spool attached to my tooth that I was caught unaware when she yanked it from my mouth with one quick jerk.

I have fond memories of that little woman with the dark hair and eyes, that could sometimes look like thunder and then other times seem as calming as a summer rain. She had a look about her that could sometimes appeared harsh but dad said that it was because of her Indian heritage and not because she was angry. As I grew older I saw it more often as she became weaker and unable to stop the disease that was destroying her body. When you are a child you don't always understand death except to know that they are with Jesus and one day we too will be there with them. She died while I was still young and her girls were just that, girls. I don't believe that any of them fully recovered from her leaving so soon.

Proverbs 27:Job, "... for better is a neighbour that is near than a brother far off. "
James 1:17, "Every good and every perfect gift is from above, and cometh down from the Father of lights, with whom is no variableness, neither shadow of turning."

There were many people that might not have had the love for Aunt Lucille that I did. There are people that may not have known her as I did. But this I know, that she loved those who were open to receive it. If there was a "Tooth Fairy" in my life it was the woman that lived next door named Aunt Lucille. She was and is a good and perfect gift from my Father above and I have been blessed.

Runaway Train

Back to an age of simpler times where time didn't seem to go so quickly and when everyone didn't appear to always be in such a hurry with some hidden agenda that must be completed. When did the clock become our enemy instead of a simple timepiece that was made to help our lives rather than control them? In the fifty years that I have lived I have seen the world step onto an invisible carousel that has quickened its' rotations until we have almost spun out of control. But, that is now and this story was in a slower and gentler time.

There was a time that whenever you went to the grocery store or filled your car with gasoline, you were given some sort of trading stamps. For those of you that don't know about trading stamps let me clarify. They were exactly what the name implied, trading stamps. You would save them in books that were available the same place you had gotten the stamps. You then put the stamps into the books and when they were full you then traded the filled books for items found in the "wish books". There were Trading Centers located in various places all over the city and if they did not have the item that you had saved for in stock, they would order it for you once they verified that you had the sufficient amount of books needed. This was the case in my story.

There were two types of stamps that were given to my parents and my mom felt the same way about the stamps as she did pennies; she threw them away. I had a totally different view of both stamps and pennies. They both were ways for me to buy things that my parents wouldn't normally buy. Each additional stamp brought me closer to the toy that I longed for in the pages of that "wish book". I had redemption books for both the S & **H** green stamps and the yellow Top Value stamps. I also had wish books for both.

My favorite stamps were the Top Value. There were more toys and fishing tackle in their wish book than there were in the book for the S & H Green stamps. One item that drove me with absolute determination was a toy train. It had an engine and four cars. The last one being a bright red caboose. The engine was black and resembled the steam engines of old. It was followed by a black coal car, orange freight car and one silver passenger car which all had authentic railroad markings. The track was a large oval much like the tracks for a slot car. The entire train was not one of the small scale so it did take up a little more space than one of the miniature HO scale trains. This could present a problem.

Mom had a rule that was set in stone, if you take it out, put it back. There was no compromise on this issue. But not to get ahead of myself let's go back to the many books of stamps that I would save for that train. Every time that mom went to the store, I searched the bags for stamps. When daddy filled the cars with gas, I was there with hand outstretched to again retrieve the stamps. Fortunately this was not an area that Sherry was interested in, so I was able to hoard all the yellow and green treasures to myself. I had calculated exactly how many books that it would take for me to get that train. I had even estimated the time with groceries and gasoline.

After many, many months of saving and dreaming the day finally came that I had exactly the right amount. I spoke with mom and daddy at dinner one night and asked them when they would take me to get my train. We had a redemption center in Riviera Beach and momma said that she would take me in a few days. How long is a few days? Too long for someone so anxious especially after waiting for my books to fill. But wait I did and then the day finally came.

The drive to the center was long or so I thought. Even though the redemption center was only about five or six miles from the house it seemed like it took forever. All the way there I looked at my wish book with its train picture and then at my books of stamps. Counting again and again to make sure that I had the right amount because I didn't want to be turned away. As mom parked the car I was already opening the door. She glared at me but it was too late, I was out of the car and halfway to the front door of the center before she had the car turned off. I waited for her to meet me at the door so I could go inside since you had to be accompanied by an adult, but it took her, or so it seemed, forever.

Once inside, I ran with stamps and catalog in hand and slapped them down in front of the clerk behind the counter. She looked from me to mom and waited until mom began to explain why we were there. I kept trying to show the picture while pushing my books of stamps across the top of the catalog. That woman would not listen to me. In total desperation I slapped my catalog down with a loud thump. Now mom and that woman were looking straight at me. Oh yeah, I had their attention now. I knew from mom's look that I was in trouble and then she made me apologize to the clerk for being so rude. I was also assured that daddy would hear of my misconduct when we got home.

With doom in the future I felt that at least I could get my train to the house before I was grounded from playing with it. I tried to look as pitiful as possible but that did not always work with mom and this was one of those non-productive times. Still after much waiting I finally saw the clerk go to the back through a curtained doorway. She was gone long enough that I began to imagine that she probably ran off with my stamps and wasn't coming back. But then the curtain moved and she emerged with a large box in her arms with the most wonderful pictures of a steam-powered train on the sides.

All the way home I sat with this prize in my lap and tried to tum it this way and that so that I could see all the pictures and writings on the outside. I really wanted to tear the box open but I knew that would be my absolute demise. Thinking that the drive there had been long did not compare to the now endless drive home. Why couldn't we live closer? As we neared the driveway mom scolded me and told me to wait until the car was in the garage and completely stopped before getting out. If she only realized that we learned that little trick from her after years of watching her walk in the front door of the house before dad ever got the car turned off.

When the engine quit I was out the door and bounding to the living room. There was the greatest floor space in that room than in any other room of the house. I stood suddenly still when I realized that I had not thought out this plan very well. I did not want to put my train out just to have to put it back into the box when I went to bed that night. I turned to face the front door and waited for mom to come through it. Not being a patient child I began to lean first to the left to see if I could see her, then to the right but still no sign. What was she doing that took her so long to come inside? At long last I saw her silhouette on the front door as she reached for the knob. Before she was even half way through the door I was pleading my case and begging her to please let me leave my train up tonight so that I could play with it first thing in the morning. I promised that I would put it in a place that would be out of the way. To my surprise she agreed.

I played with that train almost every day for months. I was allowed to leave my train set up in the living room for the entire time. Then it happened. Mom asked me to put it somewhere while the carpet was being shampooed. I couldn't find the original box to put it back into since Daddy had put it up in a closet somewhere. Definitely somewhere that I could not reach so I had to find something else to put my train into. After much looking, I found an old cardboard box in the garage and began the painstaking task of taking my train apart. First separating the cars and then separating the individual pieces of track, I carefully packed my prize into that old box and then carried it outside to the garage to set it on the top of the dryer. Certain that it was safe and out of danger I left it there until the carpet would be dry.

Then disaster struck! The next morning after checking with Mom to make sure that the carpet was dry, I ran out to the garage to gather my train. Leaping through the door I looked to the dryer and suddenly was struck with a frightful sight. The box was gone!

I ran over to the dryer and looked all around it and then began a complete search of the entire garage, including the bathroom and shower. No train! Now frantic I ran into the house screaming like a maniac as I ran to Mom's bedroom. She heard me coming and met me in the kitchen. Rapidly relating all the horrible events, she encouraged me to calm down. She would go with me to see if maybe I just overlooked the box. As we walked together back to the garage I remember feeling numb and praying that God would please help Momma to find my train.

We both looked for that box with no success until finally Mom looked at me and said that maybe Daddy had moved it somewhere else. I would need to wait for him to come home from work. That was probably one of the longest days of my young life that I remember. I tried to busy myself with other toys, games and television shows but nothing took my mind off of my runaway train. Where could it have gone? Where could Daddy have put it? Several times I went to the garage and looked up at the top shelves hoping to find a glimpse of that ragged old box. I could not understand how a box that size could just disappear.

Finally I heard the sound of Dad's tires rolling down the gravel on our driveway and I ran from the house to anxiously await him. Sometimes I am amazed that either of my parents could understand anything I spoke when I was excited. But when my discourse had ended, my Dad looked puzzled and somehow saddened. What had I said to him that would make his countenance change? He looked down at me and then kneeling down next to me he looked me straight in the eye and said, "I'm sorry. I thought that you didn't want it anymore since you put it into that old box and set it outside on the dryer". He stared straight into my eyes and made me focus on his face as he spoke. I now understand that he did that to make me see how very sorry he really was.

He spent the next few minutes explaining to me how he thought one of his co-workers, named Shorty, would really appreciate having something as wonderful as that train set. He explained how Shorty's children did not have all the nice toys and things that Sherry and I were blessed with. He told me about the joy that my train would bring to that man's children. How he would haven't been able to give such a great gift. As he spoke my entire mind only could see was the loss of something that I had saved so very long for. Something that I wanted was now gone and there was no way Daddy was going to take it away from those children. I did not care that there was a child that had less than I had or that they didn't have the chance to have the nice things I was blessed with. All I wanted was my train.

> *Jesus said in John 15:12, "This is my commandment, that you love one another, as I have loved you. "*
> *Romans 12:3-4a, "For I say, through the grace given to me, to every man that is among you, not to think of himself more highly than he ought to think; but to think soberly, according as God has dealt to every man the measure of faith. For as we have many members in one body... "*
> *Hebrews 13:17, "Obey them that have the rule over you, and submit yourselves; for they watch for your souls, as they that must give an account, that they may do it with joy, and not with grief: for that is unprofitable for you."*

The vision of a small child is sometimes limited to the space before their eyes and at that moment my focus was on the missing train that I had worked so hard to acquire. I was so focused on myself and the loss I was suffering that I did not and could not at that moment see the possible joy that was in the heart of the other child that received my train. I wasn't interested in loving someone that much nor was I willing to see that there was something here more important than I was. What I want, what I need and what I had worked for was all that was rolling around in my mind. It was not until years later that I could see that what my Dad had done was to bring a small amount of sunshine into someone else's life. A life that did not have the opportunities that I was given.

Submitting to the authority over us is not always easy and we might not ever get completely to the place where we don't question the whys and the wheres. But we have this assurance that if we have a willing heart and vision beyond ourselves realizing that we are many members yet one body, than we will be able to walk not only in peace but also with joy. It was not an easy lesson learned the day my train ran away but because of God and the gift of Grace, I begin to understand more and more how small we really are and how big God is.

The Demon Below

Sometimes in memory we see the fond images that make our hearts fill with warmth thus creating the warm fuzzies all over. Then there are the pictures that conjure fear. Such is the story of the demon fish. This is a story that any fisherman can relate if they are familiar with diverse species of fish. Uncle Jim had the most wonderful places to fish behind his house. Although we also lived on the waterway, we did not have a dock. The dock behind Uncle Jim's house was usually full with at least one tugboat and several barges, or various other types of large boats. These were great places to fish.

The dock alone was a haven for all types of fish to live around. The pilings that supported the framework of the dock and the ones that were spaced out so that the boats could tie off on both sides were covered with barnacles. There were many types of fish that would come to feed on the barnacles. Fish with teeth like Red Snapper, Sheepshead, toadfish (also called Puffers) and Jewfish were in abundance and when they came for food I would try to be there with rod and reel in hand.

Behind our house, just in front of the sea wall were some very large muck beds. Muck is a common soil in Florida that is very rich in nutrients. It is black and soft, with the exception being the areas that would not be covered with water. Muck was a large part of our lives growing up. You could always tell when there had been a muck fight because each of the combatants would be covered with black chunks in their hair and clothing. Muck was also the home of the fiddler crab.

Fiddler crabs are small crabs that are no bigger than an inch on their shells. They were usually blue or brown in color and you could always tell the males from the females because instead of having two equally sized pinchers, they had one that was enormous for their body size. The males would wave their big claw when they were trying to get the attention of the female crabs. These crabs were great for fishing since so many different types of fish enjoyed them. These were also great for scaring my sister Sherry, but that is another story.

I would often times go down to the muck beds and dig out some fiddlers to take with me to Uncle Jim's dock. Any fish that can eat barnacles will eat a fiddler crab. I was always annoyed at the little crabs when I would try to catch them. As I would approach the muck bed I could see hundreds of the little monsters lying on top of the muck sunning themselves. Then as I came near, they would scurry off into the little holes that they had dug into the muck where they lived when the tide was high. It was only at low tide that I was able to gather them for bait. With a full supply of crabs and fishing pole in hand, I started for the dock and a day of adventure.

There was a small tugboat that was tied at the dock and that was to be my fishing destination. I found the perfect place at the stern of the tug where the low sides made it easier for me to drop my line. No casting was necessary when using fiddlers as bait since most of the fish I was trying for were right under the boat. Fiddler crabs lure an assorted array of fish. Anything from red snapper to grunt were readily available. Sometimes even a barracuda would be interested in that small crustacean.

As I situated myself on board that wondrous vessel, I would imagine the places that it had been and the awesome power that that small tugboat could produce. Dropping my line in the water, I sat back and began to dream of the day that I would pilot one of these powerhouses. At eight years old I thought that that would be the ultimate job. I really believe that one of the reasons that I enjoyed fishing at Uncle Jim's was because I could spend my time exploring the many different tugboats that he would have there while they were being repaired. I would stand at the wheel and pretend that I was helping large cruise ships into port. Or aligning one of our large warships into their berth. To pilot an aircraft carrier to its dock would be a job that I knew would only be given to the most experienced tugboat pilots. That was to be me!

I'm not sure how long I spent on that small tugboat that day, but I remember not having one hit on my pole. Ready to go home, I began to reel in the line on my rod. When the line became tight, I thought at first that I was probably hooked to something on the bottom or snagged on a piling. Reeling in slowly, I could feel something on the other end of the line. There was no fight, no struggle, so in my mind there was no fish. As the end of the line was nearing the surface, I had settled in my mind that I had pulled up something from the bottom. Then it broke the surface...

There was a face so hideous, so gruesome that I screamed. Throwing my fishing rod down in the stern, I climbed back onto the dock and ran as fast as I could screaming, **"DADDY!"** As I raced passed Uncle Jim's shop I stopped and turned to look back at the place where I had thrown my pole. I was concerned that the demon being would steal my rod and reel. But not concerned enough to go back alone. Turning toward home I began to scream again. "Daddy, help me!"

Before I reached our garage where my Dad had been working, I saw him come around the corner to find where the screaming was originating. As I approached him, he immediately began size up the situation. Speaking as fast as possible I began to relate the tale of the demon from the deep that I had hooked on the end of my pole. You need to understand that from as far back as I can recall, I was under the impression that there were demons almost everywhere just waiting to get us. This of course led me to believe that I had somehow hooked into a place where they must have been hiding.

As we walked back toward the dock, my Dad explained that it was impossible to catch demons with a fishing pole. The more he tried to ease my mind the more I tried to prove to him that it made perfectly good sense to think that demons would come up from under the riverbed. After all, it is dark and murky in the shallows under those barges, what better place for a devil to hide. Still, he continued on with his stand that it was impossible to hook a demon being. I don't think I really heard what he was saying since my mind was reeling with the knowledge that he was about to be proven wrong.

As we neared the dock I could feel the fear wrapping around me like a blanket. My throat went dry, my hands were clammy and stomach was in a whirl. Daddy stepped out onto the dock and turned to see if I was following. That was a definite NO! He motioned for me to come with him to check the line on my pole. I stood firm and explained that I could see very well from where I was and that I was not coming onto that dock until he killed the monster that I had hooked.

Although fear raged in my body, I was relieved to see that my pole was still there with tip extending out over the stem of the tugboat. Daddy walked over to the fishing rod and picking it up slowly, he turned and looked at me with a face of assurance. Slowly raising the tip of the rod he focused on the object that was hooked to my line. He looked back and forth from me to the water. I was so anxious that I felt that I could almost jump out of my skin. Then it happen; he raised the rod up just enough for the monster to break the surface of the water and when it did, he screamed. Then I screamed. He turned and looked my way, threw the pole down and screamed again. I not only screamed with him, I took off running but to where? My safety was on the back of that tugboat and I was abandoning him for my own preservation. Just as I was considering that fact, I heard laughter. Not just simple quiet laughter, but the kind that rippled through the air and slapped you. I turned to see my Dad almost doubled over with uncontrolled hysteria. Now stopped completely, I did not know if it was from fear or fun that his laughter had been birthed. He looked at me and motioned for me to come to him. Still not sure what was really happening, I stood my ground until he yelled for me to come see what was creating his chuckles.

Slowly approaching the dock, I kept my eyes focusing between my Dad and the where the line met the water. Stepping out onto the dock took every ounce of courage that I could muster. At a snails pace I reached closer to the edge of the dock where the tugboat was berthed. Just as I reached the edge, Daddy looked at me and said, "Bobbie, you did not catch a demon." Reaching down and pulling the rod toward him I watched as the most hideous face again broke the waters surface.

My feet wanted to flee but the look on Dad's face held me still. As I turned to gaze at the beast that I had hooked dad began to chuckle again as he explained that it was a fish. A rock fish to be exact, or at least that's what Daddy called it. A fish that was gruesome and grotesque and down right ugly. It appeared to have weird appendages on its rather large and rounded head. With a body that narrowed down to a somewhat small tail it was an oddity to see. It still took Dad showing me fins, tail and gills to calm my fears of what I had caught.

I look back now and can laugh about the foolishness of the whole ordeal but at the time it occurred everything was very real and very scary. I did not have the knowledge then that I have today that my Heavenly Father watches out over me. My faith and trust was in the strength of my dad and what he knew of life's challenges. As big and strong as I thought daddy was, he can never compare to the gentle comfort of Jehovah, Father God.

> Romans 8:37-39, "Nay, in all these things we are more than conquerors through him that loved us. For I am persuaded, that neither death, nor life, nor angels, nor principalities, nor powers, nor things present, nor things to come, nor height, nor depth, nor

any other creature, shall be able to separate us from the love of God, which is in Christ Jesus or Lord."

It is because of the security of a loving earthly father that I am able to grasp the idea of a loving Heavenly Father. But to those who did not have the love of a physical dad, have no fear. We all yearn for the security and warmth of acceptance from a father figure. No matter how much we may deny that fact it is a part of how God made each of us. Today you stand before the face of a Father that has always loved you and even now waits to draw you into his presence. Don't wait, run to Him now just as fast as you can. You will never be turned away and nothing but you can separate you from Him.

1 Cor. 13:8, "Love never fails..."

Who's been sleeping in My Bed?

Living in a small rural community has its benefits and its drawbacks. Looking back, I see so many more benefits than I do negative things. Even now as I live in an area that is considered small town, the big city of Fort Payne, Alabama, I hear many of the youth speaking of the time that they will escape the small town doldrums. I guess that I never had that desire with West Palm Beach so close by and other surrounding cities that had vast populations with that "Big City" feel. I found myself with just the opposite desire as the city began to swallow up the small wooded area that I knew in my youth; I longed for the quiet sounds of nature.

It was a place and time that you can no longer find in Palm Beach County that surrounds the lakes and Intracoastal Waterway. Condominiums and shopping centers have filled in the woods and entire communities have been built in what was once swampland.

When I was in elementary school, Mr. MacArthur, the owner of the Colonnades Beach Hotel in Singer Island, paid an enormous amount of money to move a very old, very large Banyan tree from its place in downtown West Palm Beach. A parking lot was going to be put in the place where that lovely old tree once stood. Rather than lose it, Mr. MacArthur had it picked up by helicopter and moved to a place where he was developing a new community (in old swampland) called Palm Beach Gardens. Palm Beach Gardens is now home to the PGA National Golf Course and is also a place where much of my teen years were spent.

The woods surrounding our home were full of many types of wildlife and so were the waterways. I remember going outside one evening with my Dad and walking to the backyard toward the "canal". I was not always a quiet child, although I cherish the stillness today, and always being inquisitive, I wanted to know what Dad was looking for in the dark. As I began to question him, he put up his hand and gestured for me to be still. Standing patient and quiet was almost unbearable until he whispered to me, "Do you hear it?" Hear what? I strained my little ears to hear... a fish jump, a plane fly overhead, a boat maybe in the distance, what? With great patience Dad placed his hand on my shoulder and leaning toward me he spoke so softly, "Listen over there, and you will hear a gator." I looked toward the area that he was motioning and knew that he was pointing to a small cove near Captain Mullens' shipyard.

Captain Mullens lived directly across the waterway from us. His shipyard was really amanmade inlet that was seawalled and just large enough to fit several very large yachts, a barge or two and a big tugboat. Looking into the darkness, I listened for what, of course, felt like an eternity to only hear a dog bark somewhere in the distance. After a little while I whispered to Dad, "All I hear is some stupid dog barking and it's probably going to scare the alligator away". I could not see his smile but I am sure it was there as he explained that the sound I heard was not a dog, but was in fact the "gator". Learning the sound of a gator bark was of great benefit especially when you are fishing in unfamiliar lakes. I had no fear regarding the alligator that had somehow decided to make its home across the waterway. It was almost as if everything knew its place and most of the time they stayed in them.

That was a time you could hear a Florida Wildcat (or panther) in the night and not be fearful unless of course you had small livestock. The sounds of raccoons or opossums m your garage, or on your porches and patios, were as common as the song of the crickets in the early evening. It was a time that the locals (my family and neighbors) actually looked forward to the evening serenade from the insects, amphibians and various other creatures that would fill the night air with a symphony to announce the end of another day. Developers did not always take into consideration the extent of the loss areas would suffer as they bulldozed trees and natural woodland nesting areas. Today the Florida Panther is almost extinct and for a while the American Alligator was on the endangered list. There have been efforts made to save and/or restore the habitat, but I fear we may have waited too long.

Things we might have taken for granted are vanishing away at an alarming rate. Some things may never be restored to the beauty and the wonder that it once was, but we need to cherish and protect the existing areas for our children and their children. Even the shore line that once existed is changing, for as I write this, Florida has been hit with more devastating hurricanes in one year than in any other time recorded. Shorelines change and homes destroyed by natural forces that I am sure we somehow have had a hand in creating. God help us in our quest for happiness. As I now step off my soapbox to share a story with you let us embrace someone we love and remember that joy is still available to those who seek Him.

If you will remember back a bit about the small fiddler crabs that I used for fishing, then a new tale I will tell. The ever so small crab was great fun and a wonderful tool to use against my dear sister Sherry. As scared as I was of the dark, Sherry was probably more scared of crabs. These wonderful little creatures were a great torment to her and I was there to assist them in their quest. Okay, the quest was mine but they were an integral part, for without them I wouldn't have had much to use against her. As dumb as I was at times, I really could not believe that Sherry would fall for the same trick twice, but she did. In fact, if I waited long enough, she would even fall prey a third time. But three was all I could get away with, before she began to check things out at bedtime.

To fill you in on the details let me begin with the knowledge that when Sherry began to reach a stage in life that she was "developing" (I had no clue what that meant) she asked Mom and Daddy if she could have a room of her own. We had a guestroom and it was seldom used except to keep the ironing board and the things to be ironed. There was a wall unit air conditioner in that room but we rarely turned it on, even when we were ironing in the Florida heat. Sherry made her point one night at dinner and even made it sound like it was a good idea to me. Wow, I get my own room! That was great until it got dark and I was in there alone. Sherry was right across the very small hallway but it was a long dark hallway when the lights went out. The only thing that separated us was the bathroom between us, and a telephone seat. I am always amazed when I go antiquing and find a telephone "booth" just like the one that we had back then.

The space between our bedroom doors was no greater than ten feet but when you are scared that ten feet could look like a mile.

To take my mind off of the fears that I had, I found ways to occupy my thoughts.

Some of those thoughts led me into trouble. The lovely little crabs that lived behind our house at the waters edge were innocent in the caper but they were so important. As Sherry settled into her new room and made it clear that I was to STAY OUT of her room, I looked for ways to annoy her. Who did she think she was to tell me to stay out of her room, yet feel free to come into my room any time that she liked? She used the excuse that some of her things were still in my closet since she did not have enough room in hers. My closet ran the full length of my room and was large enough for me to keep my chest of drawers in the center. It was also large enough for me to go into with a good book when I felt insecure and unsure. But it was my closet, in my room and she needed to stay out.

If she could find reasons to invade my space then I could surely find a reason to be in hers. The only legal reason that I could find was if I had to iron something and I hated, and I do mean hated, detested and despised ironing. What other reason could I find to go in there? None that would justify my actions, so if I was going to get into trouble for being in her room then I was going to at least get some pleasure from my punishment. That is where those darling little crustaceans come into play.

On Sherry's bed was a bedspread that was very heavy. She had a full size bed, which was something special in itself since prior to that she slept in a twin bed. That large bed made a great place to hide several fiddler crabs. The males had one pincher that was larger than the other and they were more aggressive when you caught them. They were awesome partners in my crime, because when I would place them in Sherry's bed under the flat sheet that was under the heavy bedspread, the tiny crabs would just lay there with no movement. I would smooth out the covers and remake her bed so that there was no sign of her space being violated.

When my Dad built our home he installed locks on all the bedroom doors. We were told that the only time that the doors could be locked was when we were changing clothes. There was no other reason that would be tolerated or permitted. The locks did not have a key entry or the little hole that you find on many interior doorknobs today so the only way in was to break in and that was not ever to happen. But that wonderful lock on my door was what saved me from the terror across the hall when she was bent on my demise.

After placing several fiddlers in her bed, I went to my room and waited. Remembering that I was not always patient I had to find ways of occupying my time until she came to bed. I have always been an avid reader and it was something that I could do that made no sound so I could hear her approach. It really was not that difficult because she usually would either go to the bathroom or be on the telephone just before bedtime. Suddenly I heard her in the hall. Placing my book down ever so quietly, I tip toed over to the door and leaned against it with my ear. Oh how I wish that there had been video cameras available back then because I never was able to see the drama unfold. I can only imagine what went on in that room. So what follows in my idea of exactly what transpired in that room. Some of it comes from listening to her tell my parents of the ordeal and of what a horrible child I was and how I needed to be punished.

After she prepared for bed, I can imagine her ever so gently pulling back the covers. We were so different; I was a cover thrower and would almost leap into bed, she was a slider. I remember watching her when we shared a room and was amazed as to how she liked to have everything just right, or so it seemed. But back to the story... now sliding into bed and getting comfortable, she would begin to relax and drift toward sleep. Just as she was nearing that moment of slumber, the tiny little creatures realized that they were free to move. With darkness still on them they would move very slowly, but move they did.

If you've ever been camping and had a bug crawl into your sleeping bag with you or had a bug crawl on your legs, then you will understand her next reactions. Those darling little innocent crabs where caught in a fury of legs and fabric. The screams that came from the room across the hall were almost blood curdling. You would have thought that some ungodly monster had gotten into her room and was drooling over her bed. I could actually hear the sound of the covers being thrashed around as she tried to free herself from their "wicked grasp". Those were her words to describe the horror she had to endure.

When I heard her door open I stepped away from my door just in case she was able to somehow burst through it. **BOOM!** That was the sound of her flinging herself against my door with the intention of coming through it to throttle me. She grabbed hold of the knob and shook it and shook it with no avail. Now knowing that I was safe behind the locked door I began to laugh so hard that I found myself on the floor. The more I laughed the more she screamed what awful things she was going to do to me when she got inside. I could not help myself and began to taunt her in my safety. "Oh, did the little crabs scare the big girl?" She beat on my door all the more violently.

Then just as fast the fury had begun, it became almost deathly silent just as suddenly. Because I was laughing I wasn't sure if she had walked away or if she was just taking a breather. I leaned up against the door but could hear nothing. I got down on the floor and tried to look under the door to see if I could see her feet on the other side. I saw nothing and heard absolute quiet. Ever so quietly I unlocked my door and turned the knob slowly. Trying to make no noise I pulled the door toward me just a crack when... Arghhhhh, there she was. Leaping down from the telephone stand and slamming into the door as fast as she could, she was now determined to get that door open. If I could just get it shut I could again be safe. With one enormous thrust I pushed and the latched clicked. Thank God!

This time the sound was her yelling that she was going to tell Daddy and I was going to get it! I never did enjoy getting it. "It" was always unpleasant but the enjoyment I had with Sherry and those crabs was worth whatever was about to come my way. I unlocked my door and ran as fast as I could into her room to retrieve my partners in crime. After all, I could use them tomorrow for fishing. Putting them back into the jar that I had brought them in, I ran back to my room and tried to look as innocent as possible. That was not an easy thing to do, but try I did.

It did not take long before I heard the sound of their approach. Sherry was talking non-stop and to me it sounded like she was making everything seem so much bigger than it really was. Wow, did she have an imagination. I was praying that it would be Daddy coming to deal with "it" and not Momma. Mom spanked first then asked questions, but Daddy evaluated the situation before delivering the punishment. "It" would be much better if I could explain my side of the story. I had already come up with several reasons as to why I would have put crabs in Sherry's bed. My favorite story was that I was trying to keep them safe until I could use them tomorrow and after all she did have all that room in that big bed. As they neared, I decided that it really wasn't a very good story and maybe I should just tell the truth; I didn't know how the crabs got into her bed. Maybe there was a hole in the wall and they were looking for a nice dry place to stay for a while. That was going to be my story.

With the sound of my door knob turning, so did my stomach. Staring at the door as it opened I could feel my body tightening with fear. I had been caught and Sherry was a BIG tattletale. As the door swung open I saw Daddy looking irritated as he stepped into my room with Sherry fast on his heels still yammering on. It only took a look from him toward her to bring silence. He walked over to Sherry's old twin bed that was across from where I was sitting and slowly sat down. As soon as he was seated, Sherry started again with her story. Daddy again made her stop her babbling and then turned toward me. "Did you lock your door against your sister?" he asked. There was no way I could say no, so I told the truth for a change. Yes it was locked but it was an accident. I just forgot to unlock it after getting dressed for bed.

The look on Daddy's face revealed he did not believe my story. Now completely agitated, Sherry stood next to him with her arms crossed and looking from him then back to me with a look of disgust. The question finally came, "Did you put crabs in your sister's bed?" Trying not to look directly at him, I gazed around the room almost as if I was seeking for the answer in the air. Finally I told him how there could possibly be a small opening in the wall that they were able to get inside. The words had no sooner left my tongue than I knew it was the wrong approach. Again he asked whether I had put crabs into Sherry's bed but this time he was boring a hole in me with his stare. There was no way I was getting out of this without punishment.

Just as I was about to confess, Daddy spotted the jar of crabs sandwiched between some books on a shelf. Standing up and going to the bookshelf, he picked up the incriminating evidence and then turned to face me with the jar in his hand. Sherry too saw the lovely little creatures in the jar and ran from the room screaming, "I told you so!" With Sherry now in the hall, Daddy put the jar down and again faced me. I told him that I ran to save their lives when I had heard that they were hiding in her bed and I didn't want them hurt. This line was not about to be swallowed and I could see my doom was very near. As I began to confess to the crime I mixed into the story my reasons for doing such a horrendous thing to my loving sister. I tried to explain that she had pushed me into such behavior by her constant mistreatment of me. It was actually her fault that I had been driven to such measures.

With Sherry standing outside the door waiting to verify that my punishment was extreme, Daddy walked over and shut the door in her face. I almost laughed except I knew that it would bring me more trouble than it was worth. Now it was time to face the music. Daddy came back and picking up the jar of crustaceans he asked what I was planning to do with them now that I saved them from Sherry? Smiling, thinking that it might be okay, I gladly told him that I was going to fish with them in the morning. Suddenly my joy crashed to the ground as he told me that I was not going fishing tomorrow or for the next week. I needed time to learn that everything has it place and that Sherry's bed was not the place for fiddler crabs. I would have preferred a spanking because then I could have still gone fishing even if it was with a sore bottom.

As he stood to leave, he took with him my jar of crabs. Just as he reached the door he turned to face me and told me to leave Sherry and her room alone. The look on his face was a sign that this conversation was over and with that he stepped from my room. I could hear Sherry on the other side of the door questioning my punishment, and Daddy telling her that it was taken care of and she needed to go to bed. I seem to recall her asking him to please check her room for crabs that might have gotten away. I thought about locking my door after Daddy left in case Sherry tried to get her own justice but fear of getting into more trouble stopped me. As I heard Daddy walking away, I settled into bed for the night.

As I before stated, I waited a week before trying this again. Sherry and I went through the same scenario as before and again she got Daddy involved. This time my punishment was no fishing and no cartoons for a week. When you are eight years old, cartoons are a big part of your television. With too much to lose I choose to leave her alone for awhile. Sometimes time can erase enough of the pain of what you lost through correction to a point where you are willing to do the caper again. That was my case, for six months later I had to try it one more time. It was a perfect time since months before Sherry had quit checking her bed each night. For the sake of writing I would love to say that each encounter was different, but it was not. The only thing that varied was the degree of discipline that I would receive. The last time it was enough to stop the bedtime crabs and move on to something else.

> *Proverbs 6:16, "These six things doth the Lord hate: yea seven are an abomination unto Him:*
> *17, A proud look, a lying tongue, and hands that shed innocent blood,*
> *18, An heart that deviseth wicked imaginations, feet that be swift in running to mischief,*
> *19, A false witness that speaketh lies, and he that soweth discord among brethren.*
> *20, My son, keep thy fathers commandment, and forsake not the law of thy mother: 21, Bind them continually upon tine heart, and tie them about thy neck."*

Sometimes we hear words in our youth that seem stupid to our understanding. Then as we age those words become pearls of great wisdom that we too pass along. There were not many of the seven things that God hated in the scripture above that I did not commit in my torment of my sister. We all will do silly things when we are young, for that is just a part of growing. But there comes a time that each of us needs to step away from childhood and allow wisdom to develop in our actions. Never forget the exuberance of youth or the laughter for the lack of it will cause you to age with anger rather than joy. Let yesterday's errors and follies become stepping-stones to a place of understanding for you. There was no real understanding of displeasing God in my adventures at that time, but seeds planted in my youth by my parents of what the Word of God said, would one day take root. I thank God that they did!

Don't Leap This Frog

There seems to be a natural enmity between siblings from as far back as history records. Starting at the fall of man with the first brothers that were born to Adam and Eve. The division between Cain and Able is a story told to children in Sunday school as a reference that fighting is displeasing to God. I am not sure how many children really took that story to heart, since I don't remember any of my friends ever stopping a fight with their brother's or sister's in fear they might kill them and then God would be mad. I know the thought never crossed my mind when I was in the midst of battle. In fact, most of the time I was sure that God knew that I was justified in my anger for whatever reason I thought I was being mistreated.

When I was four we moved into the house on the waterway and memories of my on going war with Sherry began. Mom and Daddy were married in January of 1946 and in 1959 they were making arrangements to go out for their anniversary. Joyce Bean was hired to baby sit us while Mom and Daddy went to dinner and a movie with no children in tow. It was the first time they had been out together alone since we were born. Sherry was now eight years old and I was four and a half. Those half years are very important when you are small. People count months and weeks when you are a baby, then we go to months and years. As we age, the years run together so swiftly that we start to count decades. I am now fifty and until the day I turn fifty-one, I will still be fifty, no more fifty and a half.

Everything was now in place as the final preparations were made for the parents' night on the town. Momma made sure that dinner and snacks were ready for Joyce to reheat. Believe it or not, there was no such thing as a microwave oven available for the private home. Although they were invented, it was not something that became available for private use until the mid 1970's. If you reheated anything, it was to be done on the stovetop or in the oven. Momma even left us a *Jiffy Pop Popcorn* to be heated on the stove where we could watch it slowly expand. What fun that was. I am not sure if *Jiffy Pop* is still available today, but at that time it was the equivalent of microwaving. How we would stand with eyes wide in wonder when the foil top began to expand and the sound of the corn bursting inside the little aluminum pan. With everything in place the only thing left was to wait for Joyce to show.

Joyce was one of the children that belonged to Blackie and Mary Ruth Bean. I remember there were two sons and one daughter. They lived down the street from us at the end of Ellison-Wilson Road. Their actual address was on McLaren Road. McLaren Road was originally called Monet Road until the hurricane of 1949, when the bridge tender left the draw spans up during the storm and the winds tore them completely off. The bridge was never rebuilt and the road connecting the mainland to that small barrier island was forever closed. The county renamed the road on Pop's side after him since most all the land on that side of the waterway belonged to him and it dead-ended at his house. The opposite side of the water still carries the name Monet Road that also dead-ends when driving eastward. At the end of that road was Captain Mullens Shipyard that I understand is also no longer there.

Joyce had a younger brother that was one of my best friends growing up. His name was Jon Allison Bean but we called him Al. But that is another story so I will continue. With Joyce on her way Momma sat us down and began to explain the rules for when they were gone. Number one was to listen to Joyce and number two was NO FIGHTING! Sherry and I both promised that we would not fight and that we would listen to whatever Joyce told us to do. When Joyce arrived, Momma took her through the house and showed her where she had put our dinner and snacks for the evening. There were written instructions about reheating the items for dinner and snacks, along with what time we should go to bed. One of the last things told to Joyce was that she was not to let anyone into the house.

Hearing that no one was allowed inside, Sherry asked Momma if her friends came over while they were gone, couldn't they "please" come in to play? That was a definite NO! Looking at Joyce, Momma again stated that no one was to come into the house, NO ONE! With all the instructions given, Daddy came through the living room and stopped to thank us for letting him and Momma go on such a special evening together. It almost made you feel guilty for something you hadn't even done yet, but you then knew trouble was only a seat away with Sherry sitting next to me. It was a strange feeling to see them leaving without us. I really didn't know Joyce very well, although Sherry seemed a little more familiar with her. They were closer in age with Joyce probably being twelve or thirteen years old. She might have been older but I really don't know, when you are that small twelve or thirteen seems really old.

With everything in order, Momma and Daddy left for the evening. Remembering this was a time before cellular phones, so if anything were to go wrong, they trusted the person in charge to handle the situation. Sometimes things would happen and with so much family and caring neighbors around you could be certain someone would know what to do. It was also a time before people ran to the emergency room with every sort of ailment.

No sooner had their taillights headed down the driveway, then trouble came knocking at the door. It was Sherry's friends the Gong girls. They were two sisters that were very close in age to each other and to Sherry who lived just down the street. I don't remember their names since they were Sherry's friends and not mine. It wasn't as important to me as was to her. They stood outside the front door and waited for Joyce to answer their knock. As Joyce made her way to the door she was trailed by a shadow named Sherry. Three very large jalousie windows fronted the living room and the front door was also paneled with jalousies. It was impossible for anyone to approach the front of the house and not be seen.

Opening the front door revealed the Gong sisters. When Joyce asked then what they wanted, they explained how they had come over to play with Sherry. Oops, they must not have known that Momma and Daddy were gone and we weren't allowed to have anybody in to play. Joyce told them that she was babysitting us and that none were to come into the house. I remember them asking if Sherry could come out to play, but Joyce said, no. That **"NO"** was more than Sherry could stand. She began to plead with Joyce to please let them inside. With the saddened faces of the sisters outside and the pleading on the inside, it was more than Joyce was able to bear. She folded like a deck of cards. Sherry and her friends made every kind of promise you could imagine to our overseer about how that nothing would go wrong. They would not make any messes and would clean up where ever they played. Since Joyce stood firm on them not going outside, they had to find things to play with in the house.

I was not involved in all their fun and games, being a small child in their eyes, so Joyce played with me for a while and occupied my attention. Things really went very smoothly considering that we were breaking the parental law. As the evening lengthened, it was nearing time for the sisters to go home. Sherry begged for them to stay just a little longer. They began to think of something different to play when one of them (not sure which) came up with the idea of playing Leapfrog. This was a game that I was not familiar with and decided to watch as they played. I knew this was going to be a fun game because they had to move some of the living room furniture. Nothing major just coffee tables and the items on the coffee tables had to be moved from the center of the living room. Everything was done very carefully so nothing was broken.

With plenty of space now available, the Gong sisters along with my sister began one of the most interesting displays I had ever seen. At first I thought it was stupid for there to be such a game where you would squat like a toad while someone else crouched behind you and began to leap over you. Then it was your turn. You would then leap over the person in front of you and this would continue until... I was never sure how long they would have actually continued since the game came to an abrupt end, when I joined.

Watching from the sidelines while they had all the fun and laughter was more than I could stand. I begged to leap just once. Please, oh please, oh please! I pleaded with the Gong sisters since mine would not allow me to be a part of anything they were doing. I am not sure exactly how pitiful I looked, but eventually the sisters let me play. I waited for my tum as first one leaped over me, then another and finally the last one flew overhead and it was now my tum. As I gathered energy to make my flight, I saw that Sherry was the frog that was directly in front of me. She was the one I was to leap. Still, with all the excitement, I was ready. With her crouched in front of me I began my jump. Up I went and I thought I was really flying when suddenly I was brought down like a kite without wind. Sherry's elbow had come up and pushing me away I plummeted to the living room carpet. As I rolled away from the line of frogs, I heard Sherry fussing that she was not about to let me jump over her. After all, they weren't even my friends, why did I have to always be in the way?

Joyce could tell I was hurt and she immediately sent the Gong sister's home. When I hit the floor, I fell on my right arm, which was already swelling. Sherry taking her normal stance with the arms crossed, looked at the situation and only saw that her friends had to go home and it was my fault. Nor that she had anything to do with the problem. My right forearm was now turning colors and Joyce had determined that I had sprained it. She found my mom's large roasting pan and filled it with water and ice and made me sit at the kitchen table with my arm submerged completely in it.

While I was soaking, Sherry was fuming as she restored the living room back to the way it had been, only now she had to do it alone.

As the night progressed, Joyce kept an ice pack on my arm until bedtime. When it was time for bed, Joyce reassured us that everything would be okay. Sherry was more worried about getting caught for letting her friends in to play than she was about hurting my arm. Joyce told Sherry that it was her, Joyce's responsibility and that she would take all the blame. With that calming her mind Sherry now settled into bed. I had the twin bed across the room and was also tucked in for the night. My arm still hurt but I knew that the sooner I fell asleep then the sooner that Mom and Daddy would be home.

I am not sure how much time passed before Momma awakened me. I remember when I awoke that my right arm was resting on a pillow to the left side of my bed. That may seem unlikely but when you were a stomach sleeper as I was, it makes perfectly good sense. I did not hear the conversation between Joyce and Daddy, but I did overhear what was told to Momma as Daddy drove the car to the hospital. Joyce was staying with Sherry until they returned. He told Momma that Joyce had let the Gong girls in to play with Sherry and while they were playing a game, I tried to get involved and got pushed out of the way. It was an accident. No names were named as to who pushed me. The ride was more bearable as Momma held me in her arms reassuring me all would be well very soon. There is a comfort of being embraced in loving arms especially when you are hurting. Daddy continued to tell how Joyce thought it was only a sprain and how she soaked my arm in ice water and also kept ice packs on it while I was awake. She was unaware that I was crying in my sleep or that the swelling had increased. I understand that my cry was simply a whimper and not very loud, which makes it understandable why she did not hear it.

The next three nights were spent in the children's ward of St. Mary's Hospital. I had my arm in traction until the swelling went down and they could be set. Yes, it was broken. My sister broke my arm. In fact, she broke both bones in my forearm. Now you may think, well she really didn't mean to break your arm and I would say, true. But whether she meant it or not, she still did break my arm. I am not as traumatized about the break as I was the fact the hospital made me wear diapers while I was there. My gosh, I was four and a half years old and I wasn't a baby anymore. But they did not care of my age only the fact that I was confined to bed and it was easier than calling for a nurse. I cried more over the diaper dilemma then over the broken arm.

> *Ephesians 6:1-3, "Children obey your parents in the Lordfor this*
> *is right.*
> *Honour thy father and mother, which is the first commandment*
> *with promise. That it may be well with thee, and thou mayest*
> *live long on the earth."*

I remember being taught that commandment when I was very young. After all it is the "only" commandment of the Ten that had a promise attached to the end of it. It is an amazing thing to me that the one commandment that seemed to be hammered into us in Sunday school, was the one most often broken. Didn't we care about living long? Probably not. As we age, life becomes more precious and every day brings something to be grateful for. When youth is our companion, we feel invincible and do so many stupid things, yet do them with no fear of tomorrow not being there.

The broken arm brought many presents from family and neighbors while I was in the hospital and the cast was great for show and tell. I never found out what punishment if any that Sherry might have received for breaking my arm. I don't think that Momma and Daddy even knew that it was her fault until we were well grown. It would be quite a while before Momma and Daddy went out again without us. Their big night out ended with an over night stay in the children's wing of the hospital. I don't remember much about the stay, except the diapers and the presents. I can honestly say however that my leapfrog days were forever over, for I never again tried leaping any frog, and definitely not that one.

Keep Your Clothes On

Growing up in south Florida seems so different than many other places. The temperature was often hot and humid allowing for clothing that was light and airy. Cottons and linens were very common materials, with wool rarely being found unless it was in a gentleman's winter evening jacket. Although women's fashions were more tolerable of the warmer heavier materials, they were seldom worn. There was such a diverse array of clothing especially with the flood of polyester and nylons in the seventy's and eighty's. I can honestly say I do not like polyester and if possible, I refuse to wear any.

When I was a wee child, my mother would dress me every morning completely down to shoes and socks. I really did not like shoes that enveloped my feet and was drawn to the sandal type that was called a zorrie. Not sure if the spelling is correct since I have never heard anyone except the people in that region refer them that way. A zorrie is what is called a flip-flop, a thong or a rubber sandal. Shoes and socks were not my choice of attire. Although I do wear them today, I still feel the need for my feet to breathe. As a child I felt that I was about to die if my feet were confined to shoes.

What imaginations we have when we are young. It is a shame that some people lose that ability to dream as they age. In my mind my feet had their own set of air ducts and I could feel the very life being sucked out of them when they were enclosed in shoes. Above my shoe dilemma was the transition from diapers. I am not sure at what age I wasn't any longer wearing diapers for the change happened at a time before my recollections. I do remember training pants and this tale is during that time. Each morning I was clothed with clean garments all the way down to my toes, which if you recall had to breathe. My Mom would take great care in making sure that I was not only clean but that I had on the proper attire for the day.

As much time as Momma would spend dressing me, it seemed quite a shame I could undo her handy work so quickly. As soon as I was out the front door I had kicked off both shoes. Before stepping off the porch I was leaving behind socks, shirt and shorts. By the time my feet hit the grass I was down to my underwear which sometimes was training pants, or my newly purchased under garments; little girl panties. To call me a nature's child would be very true. I loved to be in as little clothing as possible. With my body able to breathe and feeling free to run and play I headed for one of my many hideouts.

It was not uncommon for small children to be allowed to play outside without parental supervision at that time. Although we lived right on the water and there were woods all around us, we knew what our limitations were and seldom crossed over them. My mother did not know and still doesn't know how to swim, yet that was never a concern for her since she knew that I would not go near the water without someone with me. I did however cover every area of allowed space that I could. There was much to be seen and every day brought new discoveries. Some things were constant and that is a good thing for we all need consistency in our lives.

One thing that was constant was our neighbor, Roy Richter. He and his wife, Bea lived next door between our house and Uncle Jim's. Their property, like ours, ran from EllisonWilson Road all the way to the waterway. The only property lines that anyone saw were hedges that were grown between the houses to designate where one property line started and also where the line ended. The only fences around were ornamental in nature, such as our white picket fence that was surrounding the front yard on the first house that Daddy built.

The hedges were awesome dividers with their height and density. They made wonderful places for birds to build nests, and for small children to hide. There was a place in the hedge line where our property met Roy's where the pine needles had blown under making a soft cushy place for me to sit. One of the most wonderful things in my little hideaway was the robins' nest that was just above where I sat. The mother robin seemed to not care that I sat and watched as she built her nest. It might have been because I was a daily visitor and she had become accustom to my presence. Each day I watched, as she would bring small twigs and pine needles to intertwine making a magical home for her future offspring. The time between the building of her nest and hatching of her babies was not very long, yet to me it seemed an eternity. Each day I would venture to my viewing space and wait as patiently as I was able to see if the eggs in her nest were cracking. I don't remember who told me to never touch the nest, but I did recall that if I were to disturb it in any way the mother would not return. The thought of baby birds with no mother to care for them was frightening. Enough so I never touched the nest or the surrounding limbs.

Just as a clock winds its circle daily, dividing day and night, that is how constant Roy was in tending his hedges. I would hear him coming toward where I was sitting and be as still as possible. Do I need to comment about how very hard it was for me to be still? It was extremely hard to maintain quiet. The closer he came the more I had the urge to giggle. It had become a game between him and me each time he trimmed his hedges. He would clip steadily along and whistle or hum as he went, yet never speaking. As he drew nearer to the spot where I was hiding, he would begin speaking out loud, 'I sure hope there are no animals in this hedge that bite people".

This statement had come into play because each time he trimmed the hedges I would wait until he reached the area where I was and when he wasn't looking, bite him on the leg. Okay, that sounds like I was a barbaric child. And yes I was very wild at times but I was never rabid. Which should bring great comfort to Roy since he was the person I bit the most. I never left teeth marks on his ankles and he never yelled at me for the nibble. In fact, he would jump and scream like some wild beast had just torn his leg from him. Then when all seemed to settle, he would resume his duties with the clippers and as he came closer, **CHOMP!** I bit him again.

This would go on for maybe three or four more times with Roy screaming he was being ravished by some wild animal with each bite. Then when I couldn't take it any longer I emerged from my hiding place to see Roy's face full of wonder pretending he didn't know where I had come from. We both would giggle and laugh until he decided to continue his trimming. I look back now and wonder what ever possessed me to bite this man's bare and hairy legs. The thought of doing that now is one to make me pause and give it a second thought, and maybe a third.

Roy was a great friend to a small child and he is missed. Both he and Bea hold places very dear in my heart. Bea taught me how to play *Mr. Potato Head* and *Cootie*. She had time for the little girl next door with many questions that seemed to be endless. I was introduced to a washing machine with a ringer to squeeze the water out of the wet clothes. Oh the horror stories I had heard of that ringer. Scary enough to make me stand a distance from the washer whenever Bea was using it. Bea baked cookies with peanut butter and would share them over a game of Chinese checkers. Often she let me win yet never let me know that she was throwing the game. She was a great playmate.

As I was typing this, the scripture in Matthew comes to mind about raiment.

> *Matthew 6:26-29, "Behold the fowls of the air: for they sow not, neither do they reap, nor gather into barns; yet your heavenly Father feedeth them. Are ye not much better than they? Which of you by taking thought can add one cubit unto his stature? And why take ye thought for raiment? Consider the lilies of the field, how they grow; they toil not, neither do they spin: And yet I say unto you, that Solomon in all his glory was not arrayed like one of these".*

There is innocence when seeing children run around in a diaper or training pants when they are very small. No thoughts of unclean or how disgusting come to mind. Just the beauty of the small creature that God made in His image. How wonderful is a Father who cares for every detail in our lives. Each baby robin that hatched in the nest would in time look just like it mother and father. The color was exact and the song *enchanting.* We recognize the robin by its size and color and the song it sings. If our Father God cares so much to the details of each bird, how much more does He care for you?

The days are long past since learning in that hedge. The birds and many of the people of my youth have become a warm memory. Yet a memory that has shaped who and what I have become. I would hope that Roy and Bea would be pleased with the product they sowed into so many years ago. I know that the jewels they imparted into my life have filled a space where wonder and intrigue once had been. How blessed I am to have had neighbors who were also my friends.

No Monsters Allowed

You have already heard several times how fear had been a constant companion in my youth.

Yet I have failed to give details about how that fear developed. Let me first clarify that I do not believe there were cruel intentions when my family said the things they did knowing we were within earshot. I do believe much of what was said was intentional for us to hear yet not to meant to harm, but to actually help us. Sometimes the best-laid plans can cause the most dreadful results. Follow me now as I lay a trail of the broken twigs of fear and the scattered breadcrumbs of dread that led to the house of torment I had built around myself as a child. Beware! It may sound ridiculous to you but it was very real to me.

My mother came from a small town in Kansas known as Minneapolis. It was also a place where George Washington Carver went to high school before making his mark in Alabama with the many uses of peanuts. The town was small by today's standards yet was a typical size for that day. The population, I am told, was approximately twentyfive hundred people when my mom was a child. My sister Sherry and I went with Mom in 1999 for her 55th High School reunion and found the city to have changed very little according to Mom's memory. We drove the small metropolis and found images to match the stories we had heard through the years.

My mother grew up in a world where depression was all around. She tells stories of my grandfather working for the WPA and the CCC during the time when jobs were scarce. People who lived through that period of time in our history were grateful for President Roosevelt and his plan to develop jobs for people who would have had no income without those programs. It may have caused my grandfather to work away from home some of the time, but he was able to send money home for his family. It was a time when food was rationed and often bought in bulk; such as flour and sugar. Sugar was a very closely watched commodity and was purchased only if you had a "ration card". We take so much for granted today.

It was in Kansas that the foundation of my fear was laid with my grandparents and their family's discovery of the "faith movement". It was not the "faith movement" that really caused the problem, just the sometimes bizarre ideas that were found at the fringes. I have very little knowledge of my grandfather's heritage, only that he was born in Arkansas and later moved to Kansas where he wed my grandmother. My grandmother was raised in a family where God was known as the Father of Jesus, and Jesus the savior of our souls. There was no understanding of real relationship with either the Father or the Son until the baptism of the Holy Spirit became a reality.

It was during the 1940's and 1950's that there was an explosion of faith across the nation. Men and women stepped forward in a new found boldness professing the Word of God and stating we could have and be all that the Lord had said if we would only believe. Men such as A.A. Allen, Oral Roberts, E.W. Kenyon and Kenneth E. Hagin began coming to the forefront and proclaiming the word of God with power and authority. William Branham and Kathryn Kuhlman speaking about the Holy Spirit as you would a dear and cherished friend. These were people that not only spoke the Word but had signs and wonders following wherever they went. But it was the teachings of William Branham that would tum my grandmother's world upside down.

William Branham spoke of the Holy Spirit not only as a part of the Trinity, but as one of the most important individuals we would ever encounter during this dispensation. This was the Holy Spirit of Acts Chapter two. It was a time when people were hungry for a God that could be touched and would touch us in return. Any time people are hungry for God; He will show up with more than they could ever dream. As people began seeking the presence of the Lord, and tarrying for the filling of the Holy Spirit, the anointing began to fall. Knowledge began to increase, or maybe I should say the hunger for knowledge in the Lord increased. The biggest problem then and now is that people who are hungry for God and His Word are also somewhat lazy to seek after it on their own. They want others to do the studying for them and the seeking for them so they don't have to be bothered.

Although I do not think that Grandma or her mother, Grandma Jackson, were slack in their devotion to the Word of God, for I have heard stories of how they both were constant in their prayer life and studies. Mom tells the story of how she could hear Grandma praying as she approached their home after school. These were women of faith who hungered to know more of God than they had before. They didn't seem to suffer from the same disease, and I do mean "disease", that we seem to be afflicted: The disease of "terminal laziness". It is a disease that can not be detected unless there is a thorough examination. Just as David in Psalms 139:23 cried, *"Search me, O God, and know my heart: try me, and know my thoughts: (24), And see if there be any wicked way in me, and lead me in the way everlasting. "* I would love to say I have never suffered with a case of the lazy's, but that would be a lie. I too have tried to get my understanding of God and His Word by just listening to the diligence and hunger of someone else. Won't happen. Until we are willing to seek Him diligently ourselves we will never see the fullness in our own lives. But I am getting away from my story...

My grandmother loved the Lord and devoted most of her life to ministry. She and Grandpa were the pastors of a small church in West Palm Beach, Florida called the Christian Training Centre. Although Grandpa's name was known as Rev. Ray, it was Grandma that carried the anointing to deliver God's word. Grandpa took care of the administrative side of the church and was the appeasing side for all those that felt a woman had no place in ministry. I was told I was two weeks old when I attended my first service there. If you are wondering what happen to Kansas let me explain, after Momma married Daddy they went to live in Florida where my dad's home had been. It was not long before Grandma and Grandpa followed them to the Sunshine State.

In a short amount of time, my mom's two sisters and their husbands also moved to Florida and built homes nearby in Juno. Later Aunt Lillian and Uncle Bud moved to the southern end of West Palm Beach right next to where the city later built Drear Park Zoo. Grandma and Grandpa bought property off of Okeechobee

Road, later changed to Okeechobee Boulevard, and lived in a two-bedroom apartment above the church. Aunt Dolores and Uncle Freeland built a home right next door to our house in Juno. This is where everyone physically was when I came into the world. The spiritual location is much different. I can not tell of each family and what was in their hearts, neither can I make assumption as to motives, but as I share the next few bits of knowledge please listen with an open heart.

As a small child my mother was bound in a prison of fear. A fear that was so real she was in constant torment and terror. The fear she would blaspheme the Holy Spirit was so out of control until she would be driven almost to the very edge of sanity. She has related stories of washing dishes over and over because somehow she felt she was in danger of blasphemy. She would cry and seek God over things she thought she might have said or done that would have made her cross that invisible line of blasphemy. No one explained what blasphemy of the Holy Spirit was or what it was not. All she knew was that she had better be careful or she might just do it accidentally. This was a fear she carried with her almost all through her life. Even as an adult she would go into the master bathroom of our home and sit on the floor and cry out to God in fear of nearing that line.

My grandmother knew of her fear yet did not understand blasphemy any better than Momma. They only remembered Brother Branham disobeyed God somehow and his life was cut short. If a man of God who walked in the power and anointing as brother Branham had could step over a line to shorten his life and ministry, who could be safe? This is the message I believe that laid the foundation of fear and dread. I need to interject at this time that you can NOT accidentally blaspheme the Holy Ghost. It is something that you do willfully and with no care of God or the Holy Spirit. Any person denying Christ and the sacrifice He paid does so with willful intent. For to know of the price paid and to reject the gift of God, is blasphemy.

I don't know when or how long it was before Grandma and Grandpa began to see the power of controlling people with fear. I do remember when I was very young how the words were used, "God will get you" if someone was not doing what was thought they should. Fear has a twin called manipulation and the two works awfully, and I do mean awfully well together. Manipulation is rampant in the church today. It fills our prayer life as we pray for others to do what we think they need to do, not always what the Word says they should do. If your prayers are not Word based they are probably manipulating. You may not know everything about that person you are praying for and you surely do not know their heart for only God is the discerner of the thoughts and intent of the heart.

With that little bit of insight you should have a better understanding of the root of my fears. My fears were not of crossing the invisible line of blasphemy or of displeasing my Father God. Number one, I really didn't know God as my Father and secondly, the Holy Spirit was something for grown-ups. The seed of my fears were demons. With the revealing of the Holy Ghost and His empowerment, people began to deal with spiritual battles and if it was spiritual it must be a demon or devil. I would listen to stories of devils possessing people and talking through them. The story of the man of Gadarenes was heard often of how this one man had over a thousand demons inside controlling his life and of Jesus sending them into a herd of swine. Not into the pit, but into a herd that drowns and then releases all those devils into the air to attack someone else. Good grief! Were we ever going to be safe?

Then there were stories of local people and their deliverance from demonic possession but those stories were of people with super human strength and voices that were guttural. Tales of one man full of demons overpowering six and seven others while they were forcibly trying to rid a spirit from that one man with loud voices and physical strength. You can scream at the devil all day and never lose anything but your voice. Or you can speak a Word in faith and know he must heed the Word of God and the power of the Blood of the Lamb. Of course it was more dramatic to see the physical confrontation with a demon possessed person than it would have been to just do what Jesus did, speak a word.

We have become such an entertainment driven society that we would rather see drama such as that or see people acting in the flesh. I better stop now before I step onto to another soapbox.

Hearing about demonic attacks and devils lurking everywhere just waiting to find a way into your house or your body was block by block building the room of fear where I lived. I felt fairly safe in the daylight because I knew they were afraid of the light. I did not understand the light was in reality Jesus. All I knew was they came out at night and that was their time of power. It did not help that Sherry really liked to watch scary shows and I usually was watching them with her. I call them scary, but by today's standards the shows of that time would be a joke. Shows such as the original Dracula, Frankenstein and the Mummy. Movies in black and white depicting horrors my mind was well able to see in full living terrifying color. Yeah, the blood may have been a dark gray but I saw it in deep red. Vincent Price was a very scary man and I knew if he was in the movie, my dreams that night were doomed. There was one show he was in called "The Wax Museum" or "The House of Wax" that was the cause of me rearranging the furniture in my bedroom. Any lines on the ceiling could allow a hidden guillotine to take off my head. I wasn't taking any chances so my bed was moved. It may sound foolish to you but to me they were very real.

When I went to bed at night, even during the time that Sherry and I shared a room, I had to have the closet light on. One of the three sliding doors had to be opened just a crack so I could see if there was anyone moving around inside. The drapes had to be closed and I made a complete check every night under the beds and inside my toy chest to make sure all was clear. I was terrified someone or something would try to come up through an invisible door under my bed, or maybe through my toy chest. The fear of seeing eyes peering at me through the window was enough to have my covers pulled way up over my eyes and ears. Any opening of my body might be used as a doorway for some unearthly and definitely ungodly creature to attack. Oh what an imagination! But imagine or not, to me it was all very real and I was in danger.

The fears of a small child can be enormous. The worst thing about fear is that many of us never learn to overcome the terror. We rationalize why we are afraid to a point where we don't feel quite as scared as we did. If we can come up with a reason for our fear even if it is ridiculous, we would rather have that reason than no reason. It is a sad thing to me how we push ourselves to face fears that we should never have to encounter. One example of this is my nephew John. John was a sweet young man with a heart as big as the outdoors, which is where you would usually find him. We often joked that John never learned to walk, because it seemed he hit the ground running and never stopped. He was an inquisitive little boy full of questions and never short on giggles. And then he started school... What a travesty when we create a society where everyone has to be just alike. After he began his journey through life with the other school children, he found that he was not normal if he did not watch, and like scary movies. His friends were cruel about his not liking *Friday the 13th* or *Halloween* or whatever of the killer/slasher type movies they were watching. What I really wonder is where are the parents of these children and why are they allowing their offspring to be fed with this kind of fodder?

But back to John, he asked his parents to please rent for him all the scary movies that they could so he could become just like his friends. This is the same child that I had to leave the movie *Tron* because he was scared of aliens. We did leave the theater mid movie because I would not make him sit through something that I thought was okay but to him it was complete terror. Only two years later he was sitting in front of the television and VCR watching a blood feast of horror shows, just so he could fit in and not be made fun of anymore. Why do we not guard our young and their tender hearts? Why do we want them to be as spiritually perverted as we have become? What may not scare you can cause fear and dread in another.

To cope with the many things we encounter in our walk in this life we either learn to lean completely on God, or we learn to harden our spirit and heart against the daily obstacles we face. My family did not mean harm in freely using the "God will get you" method, yet it was a tool that was utilized to steer us the way they thought was correct. You must understand also that manipulation was not understood by those involved. I believe manipulation is an acquired trait passed down from generation to generation. If it is used in your families please break the chain now.

I was so ingrained with the "God will get me" doctrine, along withwdemons and devils under every rock and bush, that it has taken years and many tears to reach a place where I can stand with total confidence knowing God has me in the very palm of His hand. No one told me of the many promises given to me by my Father or of my covenant rights. I really did not have an understanding of a Father that loved me not because I was good but in spite of the fact without the Blood of Jesus I would never be righteous. He loved me while I was dirty, while I was lost in my own confused mess.

> *Romans 5:6-8, "For when we were yet without strength, in due time Christ died for the ungodly. For scarcely for a righteous man will one die: yet peradventure for a good man some would even dare to die. But God commendeth His love toward us, in that while we were yet sinners, Christ died for us".*

I was not aware of a God that loved me while I was still unclean. I thought I had to clean myself and try to live without sin before He would look my way. I had been told that the only prayer He hears is a repentant prayer. No one explained how He wanted to be involved in every part of my life. Often the "church" today tries to do God's work when reaching to the lost. The best I have heard it explained is this: We are only to lead them to Christ, not clean them also. My Pastor once told it as a fisherman with our job being to hook the fish or potential brother and God's job to clean, scale and gut them. God is the only one that can change a heart and transform the spirit of man.

I now teach Sunday school for young people seven to twelve years old and it has become my mission in life to make them aware of a Father that loves them beyond all the mistakes they will make in their lifetime. A Father who stands with His eyes always on the horizon looking for their return with arms open and longing for their fellowship. It is unrealistic to think that we won't make mistakes, but it is vital to know there is a place where all things can deal with as long as we know our place at the Father's house. In my fiftieth year the Word of God has set me free from my fears of childhood. For in the Old Testament I found a word in one of the most unlikely books I would have ever thought. We know to look in Deuteronomy 28 to find the blessing promised. Also Joshua 1, along with many places in Genesis where God makes covenant with Abraham as to what he could expect from a covenant partner. There are many other books that speak of the promises of God toward those who love Him. But the book known as the "book of the law", Leviticus was where I found liberty.

> *Leviticus 26:3-6: "If you walk in my statutes, and keep my commandments, and do them; Then I will give you rain in due season, and the land shall yield her increase, and the trees of the field shall yield their fruit. And threshing shall reach unto the vintage, and vintage shall reach unto the sowing time; and ye shall eat your bread to the full, and swell in your land safely. (Check this out) And I will give you peace in the land, and ye shall lie down, and none shall make you afraid: and I will rid*

evil beasts out of the land, neither shall the sword go through your land."

Do you see that! I am supposed to lie down and not be afraid because all the evil beasts are going to be taken care of by my Father. He will take care of the eyes peering in the window and the creatures trying to come out from under my bed or out of the closet. He will not let anything get me as long as I love His ways. Welcome all you weary and scared children. Welcome all kids from three to one hundred years old to a place of safety and hope. Don't be scared anymore for your Father stands on the horizon with open arms waiting to embrace you with His warmth and love. There is no safer place than in the Father's arms. Breathe deep and long for your hope is but a whisper away... Father save me! Just that fast and just that easy is the way to peace and comfort. Though your life look hopeless and your future looks bleak, remember there is a door called Jesus who gave it all so you too could find your way to the Father's house. Welcome home!

The Sound of Terror

What is it that makes your skin crawl? What causes you to want to jump into bed with the covers pulled up over your head? We each have something that makes us want to run in complete panic. Each of us may face a different fear or anxiety than the person next to you, but face them we do. Having given a background of the fears I have faced let me share with you that I did not fear much else. I loved to play with bugs and lizards, garden snakes and really big grasshoppers. The fear of snakes did not have a place in my life until I was much older. That understanding happen when my dad was building our house on the waterway. It was there I was told that not all snakes were as my dad called it, friendly.

The foundation of the house had been poured and the workmen were waiting for the concrete to set. The block footers of the house rose several inches above the newly poured floor and once the cement had dried, the workers often sat on the block wall while having their breaks or eating lunch. As stated before, while Daddy was building this house I was very much under foot and never out of the way. When the men stopped working, I stopped playing. When they had lunch, I had lunch with them and where they sat, I sat too. This one day as we were sitting for lunch there were several boards lying on the floor of what was to be our new garage. It was there that we perched on the blocks forming the footers for the walls soon to be erected. As we ate our lunch I saw movement near the edge of the pieces of wood where the workmen's feet were resting. I had left my sandwich and began poking at the tail of whatever was hiding. Soon Daddy noticed my activity and stopped to see what I had found. It was my first encounter with a water moccasin and Daddy made it quite memorable. In one swift motion he flipped over the boards and swept me out of danger. He lifted me so fast I actually remember feeling exhilarated by the movement. Almost like a ride at the fair.

The next thing that happened was almost gruesome to a small child who loved to play with green snakes. Daddy picked up a shovel and brought it down right behind that snake's head. Boom! The snake began to wiggle and shake, but Daddy was quick to hit him again. The fight was not over until that pretty black snake had lost his head. Not only did he lose his head, but it was separated from him completely. Daddy had one of the workmen dig a hole and bury the head. Not the whole snake, just his head, how weird was that? I later was told that if someone had come in contact with the fangs of a poisonous snake, even though they were dead, it could still prove fatal. So much to learn when you are growing up. I had no fear of that thick black snake because it had no rattles and up until that day, the only snake I knew was bad had rattles on the end of its tail. Daddy told me that morning to avoid all snakes unless they were green, and believe it or not; I did.

There were many creatures in South Florida that could be fatal if you had an encounter with them. However, the creature in this story has not been known for killing a human, unless it would be from the sheer terror they created with the sound of their gnarly hideous pointed legs. Or maybe it would be the clicking sound you could hear from their claws. Then there was always the startle factor, much like a snake in this area, for just when you think all is well... Argggh, right in front of you is the multijointed, round bodied land crab. If any human were to die from an encounter with one of these, it would have been Sherry. She had a fear of every type of crab. Size didn't matter for her fear was all the same, really big. In fact, she was scared of anything with claws or pinchers.

The land crab was similar to the tiny fiddler crab with the same amount of legs and claws. They both had eyes on the top front of their shells that were at the ends of what appeared to be short muscular tubes. The eyes could work together or independently and would disappear into a grove at the first sign of danger. One difference I noticed was in the claws. The male fiddler crab had one very large claw and one small claw, where the land crabs claws didn't seem to designate male or female. It seemed every land crab had a big and little claw regardless of gender. Not being a crab expert, I could be wrong. What I am sure of is the land crabs were a guaranteed visitor in the months of April and October of every year.

During those two months we had what was known as high tides. This is not the low and high tides that occurred naturally every six hours, but a tide or water shift where the high tides were much higher than normal. It was also during this time of year when rip tides were more dangerous along the shore. April was a very challenging month for us as kids. It was warm enough for us to go swimming, but the water was too dangerous for us to head to the beach. Daddy allowed us to swim in the "canal" in April usually during the low tides, since there was less risk of being swept away by underlying rip currents. The ocean was totally off limits. It was a real challenge for surfers during both months with the unusually larger waves caused by the higher water table. October was a different story in one factor only. The month of September was a time when the sea was full of sharks. I seem to recall the Jaycee's having a shark rodeo, but not sure if it was at that time of year. Between the rip tides and the sharks you had to either be borderline crazy or maybe just had the idea those factors did not apply to you, therefore you were exempt from danger. Having been caught in a rip current, I can tell you no one is exempt.

It was those two months that forced the usually elusive land crab from their homes to come to live at our house. As the tides rose along the shoreline of the Intracoastal Waterway the water began to flood the crabs' homes and they began searching for shelter above water. Although they lived near water, they were not water crabs; thus the name "land" crabs. I never did, nor do I now know the real name of that type of crab. Maybe their official name is Land Crab. As they searched for higher ground they found their way into our garage, hedges and places around the house where they could hide from predators. The ones making their home in our garage were the ones guaranteed to make every hair in your body quickly stand on end.

Any time of the day you could walk through the garage never fearing that something was watching you. The months between April and October were just enough to allow our minds to forget the seasonal arrival of our houseguests. Then just when you thought it was safe to go outside you encounter the sound of "click, click, click". Actually it was many more clicks but memory of the horrible sound makes me want to shorten their sound of alarm. Alarm, yes. You see they were terrified of us. Not sure if they were more terrified than we were of them but I do know they were scared of humans. When you look at the big picture of a large two-legged person towering over that tiny crustacean, it would seem natural for the tiny crab to quake in absolute terror. Yet it is the very large animal to scream in fear. I guess it goes back to the story of the elephant and the mouse, or the lion and the field mouse. Large powerful animals seem to tremble at the very sight of the tiniest life form. So is the nature of fear. Fear has no size limits. What may seem silly to one person will completely unnerve another.

The fear that griped my sister would cause her to step from the front door very slowly with watchful eyes for any signs of movement. There was a span of about eight to ten feet of the front porch that had to be crossed before entering the garage. There were very few places for the crabs to hide on the porch, so the place most likely for an encounter was the very full cluttered garage. The garage was a perfect place for a homeless crab to find shelter. The large twocar garaged door was usually open exposing walls that were lined with shelves, tools, lawn equipment and anything that had no other place. The washer and dryer were away from the wall just enough to provide a cozy hideaway. Then there were the lockers, which stood six inches off the floor and again made a great place to find refuge.

The lockers were from Palm Beach High School when they renovated years before and my dad brought some home to use as a great place for storing extension cords, old clothes and anything that just needed to be tucked away. They were olive green, battered and stood about six feet tall. It was here that most of Sherry's fears would focus as she entered the garage. She stopped at the doorway and would peer into the vast expanse with eyes straining to see movement and ears alert to the first "click". I was not any help to her in overcoming this phobia for as she would step into the garage and make her way almost halfway through, I would scream out, "There's one!" To this day she still has the fastest feet I have ever seen. She could cross that concrete floor in what looked like two hops. For a family that has demonstrated complete clumsiness, it is still a wonder to me how she was able to perform such feats without totally collapsing on the floor. Fear seemed to be the stabilizing factor in what could have been the most comical ballet ever seen. Fear and determination to escape those monsters under the lockers gave her unnatural abilities.

I don't remember many things causing Sherry to fear, at least not like I did. But I was confident of the twice a year event of the invasion of the crabs to yank her chain just enough that she appeared to have some form of vulnerability. It made me feel just a bit more normal. It also gave me something to torment her with even if it were only a small time span. As if her fear of crabs was not enough, I would sometimes hide under the car and wait for her to come through the garage. Knowing she would walk as close to the car as possible to avoid any contact with the creatures hiding along the wall, I would wait ever so quietly. Just as she would step in front of my hiding place, with her eyes scanning the walls, I would reach out and touch her legs. I had learned through trial and error to use a twig or small branch instead of my hand to startle her. The first time I used my fingers to lightly brush against her bare leg and found I was not a fast as her feet. She came down on my hand with such force I thought it was broken. The swelling of my stomped appendage was also proof of my violation. There was no way I could say I did not do it with physical evidence throbbing at the end of my arm.

The trauma caused by touching her leg always gave me just enough time to escape her wrath. She would scream and dance, a movement I like to call the "dance of the claw". A step she alone developed thinking she had actually been touched by the creepy crustacean before realizing the crab had been me. Fortunately for me, she had to regroup her thoughts before coming after me. That gave me a small window of time needed to escape the "Wrath of Sherry". It was always a more blessed thing to have the wrath of Daddy then it was to get pounded by her. Although I am certain she would have much rather punished me every time for each transgression.

As we grew older, she became more aware each April and October to watch for my hiding places. She held to the center of the walk area instead of toward the car or wall to avoid both crabs and Bobbie's. The game became boring and had to change. I went from hiding in places to scare her to hiding crab claws anywhere I knew she would be. The claw in the pillowcase, or hiding a claw attached to a hanger in the closet or in a pocket. These were wonderful and unexpected changes. Years later I would even hang one from her steering wheel, a place unnoticed until she was fully in the car. That time I thought she would rip the door off that old car trying to escape "The Claw". As she yanked and pulled on the door handle, she was yelling out all the horrible things she was going to do to me when she got free. By the time she was free, I was no where to be found. Yes, I am smiling while typing this as all the old joys of torment come flooding back into my mind. This is not a place where I would like to liken myself to Satan, but it does appear that in the flesh we do pursue many of the same tactics.

> 1 Peter 5:5-8, "Likewise, ye younger, submit yourselves unto the elder. Yea, all of you be subject one to another, and be clothed with humility: for God resisteth the proud, and giveth grace to the humble. Humble yourselves therefore under the mighty hand of God, that He may exalt you in due time: Casting your cares upon Him; for He careth for you. (this is the biggie) Be sober, be vigilant; because your adversary the devil, (or your darling younger sister) asa roaring lion, walketh about (or hideth under the Buick) seeking whom he may devour: (or scare the fool out of).

Okay, I have taken a few liberties with that scripture and hopefully you realize that all in the parentheses is in fact, my interjection and not the Word of God. There was no concept of submitting to my elder, that being Sherry, or even the faint idea of humility. What was that all about? The only elders I knew were Momma and Daddy and people around their age, certainly not my sister. After all, she was just a punk kid like me and not someone to be respected. I may not be the devil, but I sure did a lot of devilish things in my younger years. They say with age comes wisdom and I can say that to be true. I wish sometimes the wisdom came sooner and I did not have to wait until I was halfway through my journey here to seek it as a constant companion. Solomon wrote the Proverbs and instructed us continually to seek wisdom. Wisdom rooted and grounded in the thoughts and precepts of God.

Proverbs 3:13, "*Happy is the man that findeth wisdom, and the man that getteth understanding.*"

I understand now how wrong I was to play on the fears of another. I did not see any wrong while in my youth for all was a game played at someone else's pain. I thank God there was no lasting damage, although she still will not sit next to me when I eat crab legs or lobster. I thank God that she and I no longer look to pound each other and the laughter we hear now is shared and not at one another's expense.

Time in a Bottle

We live in such a different world today than what it was when I was a child. If you were to look at just the technological advances it could boggle your mind. In the fifty years I have lived, I have seen monumental historical events that are counted among some of the most memorable in the last century. The first man landing on the moon kept us glued to a black and white screened television set for hours waiting to see Neil Armstrong stepping out with, "one small step for man, one giant leap for mankind". It was a time of conflict in Vietnam and turmoil at home with protesters filling streets and colleges. A war that sent young men into a battle that was televised bringing the horrors of death into our homes. "Draft dodgers" were counted both as cowards and heroes depending on your opinion of our involvement.

History filled with hatred and unrest. From the assassination of John F. Kennedy, Martin Luther King, Jr. and Bobby Kennedy to the death of Elvis it seemed time continued to march on regardless of the dark days our nation faced. The sixties brought a new culture to our fashion with a mix of tie-dye and army green. It was the rage to wear an army jacket and in our area a shoe called "desert boots". Hip huggers and bell bottom pants fought for a place along side mini skirts and halter tops, and America's youth was beginning to move to a different beat.

There was a place where half a million young people gathered for a three day event that left a mark on the music world as never before, or since, a place called Woodstock. We watched as drugs and "free sex" became the rage with violence following in its wake with a voice crying Peace and Love. Then there was the day the Beatles came to America. The sound of Liverpool filled the airwaves and the hearts of young girls from shore to shore with a longing to catch a glimpse of the Fab Four. Music evolved from the bubble gum sounds of the fifty's to the psychedelic groups in the sixties. Groups not only encouraging drug use, but giving the impression they had to be stoned to perform. People transforming sounds, such as Jimi Hendrix with his innovative guitar. Then the seventies arrived with a mix of rock that ran from Fleetwood Mac and Aerosmith to Led Zeppelin and Black Sabbath. Carol King, James Taylor and Billy Joel came with a softer sound. Gladys Knight and the Pips, along with Al Green and Barry White competed for airtime alongside disco mania.

The pounding pulsation's of the eighty's and ninety's saw a change in country music. Country music was once defined by the sound of the steel guitars accompanied by voices that were unmistakably "country". Johnny Cash, Loretta Lynn, Roy Acuff and Hank Williams sang of the heartache of living and the twang in their voice made you feel the agony they knew. George Jones and Tammy Wynette, Conway Twitty and Loretta sang songs and drew you into their world by telling you a story you could relate to. We have gone from music with heart, to heartless and demeaning lyrics that have betrayed our society and perverted our youth. The changes from Motown to disco, punk rock and rap, to head banging heavy metal, have lead us forward in a succession of pounding rhythms and dancing feet; and dance we did.

Time has marched forward to a place where computers can now be carried in one hand and contain more knowledge and capabilities than the monstrous wall sized units of the 1960's. We have become mobile as never before yet it appears to this writer that we have also become more separated. How ironic that we can be connected via cell phone and Internet in seconds, ways once unimaginable, yet we have become isolated emotionally. I have watched as President Nixon was caught in Watergate and almost impeached. Celebrated with our nation during the 1972 Olympics when Mark Spitz brought home seven gold medals, and mourned with the world as we watched the horror of the PLO's invasion of the Israeli team's dorm knowing that tragedy was destined.

Sometimes I sense George Orwell looking at our world and nodding his head in an "I told you so" manner. We have definitely become a society of new speak and if there ever were to be a Big Brother, it would and could be now. The RFI (radio frequency identification) chips will probably be available very soon worldwide and then when it is implanted in your flesh, you can be tracked just like Onstar. Sure would make sneaking away or hiding a thing of the past. But do we want to be monitored so closely? Do you want people tracking you down no matter where you are, never knowing if they were friend or foe? And it would definitely make it impossible for someone to hide from the **IRS**. Sometimes the future looks scary and other times I embrace it with wonder and eager anticipation.

During the 1970's and 80's I watched a new culture emerge that had been hiding in the shadows and closets. I learned that the word "gay" did not mean merry, bright or lively but it had become the word defining a group of people choosing to live a lifestyle of homosexuality. With the rise of same sex unions we begin to see a greater number of people dying from AIDS. Before the 1980's I had never heard of AIDS or HIV. Had no understanding of any diseases transmitted sexually except Syphilis and Gonorrhea and there were classes on Human Sexuality during High School that showed us how to prevent transmittal of those STD's. Yet it was a difficult time with mixed messages. On one hand you had the "how to not catch a STD" and on the other hand there was "if it feels good, do it". Then you wonder why our generation was so confused and unfocused.

I was blessed to live during the Reagan administration and see a man stand for what he believed in and not back down in the face of terror. I've seen our President appear broken by the tragedy of the space shuttle *Challenger* and watched as he stood strong when our nation trembled in 1987 when the stock market took it's lowest dive since the Great Depression. This was a man that held our nation together at a time of breaking apart. He was also the man that told Mikhail Gorbachev to tear that wall down, in reference to the Berlin Wall; in 1989 the wall came down. The Reagan years, though filled with many challenges, were years of hope and belief in a better tomorrow. I cried along with the nation on the day he died. He was a great man and a great president and we are the better for having shared life with him.

From a man of integrity to a president with none was quite a transition. The scandal in the White House should have been no surprise with the tumultuous history of Mr. Clinton. He not only let down his family, but an entire nation that looked to his office for stability and honor. Then for the ordeal to go on for such a lengthy time with his continual denial to what would later, in fact, be truth, was criminal. He wasted our time and our nations money proving to the world you don't have to be a "man of your word" to be a leader. This was, in my opinion, a dark moment in the history of this great country. So much that once again we were on the verge of impeachment of our top official. I actually felt shame and pity for the entire Democratic Party that he represented. Thank God those days are behind us and we can and have moved forward.

In just the last ten years we have seen terror strike our nation. First the Oklahoma City Federal building was bombed hurtling a nation into grieving and fear. Will it happen again? The lives lost were not related to me, yet I felt horror and pain as they showed the rubble knowing that underneath were mother's, father's and someone's brother or sister. What if it was my own under there? Bombs became the weapon of choice in many attacks following, such as Atlanta's Olympic Park and the Birmingham Abortion Clinic. Our own people were attacking us, so the September 11th destruction took this nation by complete surprise.

The idea of flying planes into the Twin Towers was something you might envision on a movie but not in real life. Using a fully loaded passenger plane as a weapon of destruction is inhuman. People, American people to be precise, to kill other American's is stuff horror stories are made of, not something in reality. What manner of men were these that live to die? The only good thing to come of the 9/11 tragedy was the hearts of American turned, if only for a short time, to God. It reminds me of the shark movies;

as soon as there was no sign of a shark, it was time to go back into the water. Beware, sometimes sharks swim deep and you may not see a fin, but they are still there just waiting for an opportunity to strike. This is the same way with terrorist; you may not see them openly but given the right opportunity, they will strike again.

How fortunate we were to have a man like George W. Bush in office when tragedy struck. Although you knew he was hurting just as all America, he stood tall and strong in the face of adversity and gave us words of hope. In a time of fear and dismay he spoke to the hearts and the very spirit of America. Not being a fool, I know President Bush is not perfect, yet I also know that he doesn't have to be. He claims to know Jesus Christ as his savior and that makes him righteous. Our prayers should be with whoever is in the office of President, and with his administration. It is our duty to both God and to our country whether you like the man or not, to pray.

Oh how I sometimes wish for simpler times. Do you think in fifty more years people will look back at today and dream of this time as a time of simplicity? Could our morals possibly get any worse or man become more perverse and decadent? I am sure of this one thing; if God does not intervene in the direction man is headed, then we will surely destroy all that is decent and good. There is no good thing in man except he get it from God.

James 1:17, "Every good gift and every perfect gift is from above, and cometh down from the Father of lights...

I started off with the mindset of sharing with you the story of collecting bottles and somehow got off course with a mini history lesson. I guess change is the one thing we can all be certain will happen. Not all change is bad and not all is good; but change will come.

Change today is the recycling centers all over our nation that hopefully are helping us to create a better tomorrow by not being the excessively wasteful country we have been in the past. Plastic has replaced glass in everything from the bottles we feed our newborns to the parts in our automobiles. As wonderful as plastic is the one thing it is not is biodegradable. It is however, recyclable and can be used over and over again. It has not always been that way, and this is actually where I was headed before my brief walk down memory lane.

When I was a child, in the early sixties, all sodas were packaged in glass bottles. The bottles were either six or, if I remember correctly, ten- ounce bottles. The twelve and sixteen-ounce bottle did not come until I was in my teens. The greatest flavor seems to come from the little six- ounce bottles of *CocaCola* and there was nothing to match it, not even to this day. Glass was heavy and took a lot of space in the landfills and in your garbage cans at home. This might be the reason soda bottles came with a deposit attached to them. It was a way to not only protect our land but to re-use the bottles. The glass was very thick, creating the expression, "coke bottle glasses" to anyone wearing eyewear that appeared thick and rounded.

The weight of each bottle was almost the same as the contents of the drink. It made it very difficult for a little person to carry more than two at a time. When your hands are small, one bottle in each hand is all I could manage. This made my little red wagon one of my greatest tools in my venture. It gave me the capability of carrying up to six, six packs of bottles without stress. Thirty-six bottles would give me back seventy- two cents at two cents a bottle and that bought a whole bunch of things for me to either play with or to munch on.

It was a time when you could buy a soda for ten cents, with a twocent deposit, and a comic book for the same price. Candy bars were larger than the standard bar of today and still only cost a dime. Needless to say, there were still penny candies available and ice cream bars also five or ten cents. The bags of toys that hung on the display were never more than adollar and if there were one I really wanted, then I would save money every week until I had enough. My dad had shown Sherry and I about putting salted peanuts into a *CocaCola* and enjoying them together as you sipped. If I drank my soda at the store then I didn't have to pay the deposit and that was something I did often. Not because I was trying to save money but because I was always busy looking to see what else I wanted to buy.

My parents were not my supply of soda bottles to return. We did not have cokes in the house usually unless it was a special occasion. It was always a special treat to get a soda when we were out. I still remember the Dr. Pepper bottles with the clock on it with numbers to signify the best time to drink; which really was anytime. Mountain Dew came on the scene with some hillbilly guy taking big swallows and declaring to the world, "Yahoo, Mountain Dew, it will tickle your innards". We had to try any drink capable of tickling our innards. Then there were the wonderful fruit flavors of Nehi Orange and Grape sodas. I honestly believe the drink formulas have changed over the years or my taste buds have no memory, but somewhere there was a definite change.

Getting back to Momma and Daddy, I was not given a lot to work with because of the absence of sodas purchased at our house. We drank *Kool-Aid* or milk, water or orange juice and knew better then complain about our choices. Daddy never reminded us of the starving children overseas, but he did explain how precious water was and how many people had to walk miles just to get a drink from some community well. Parents really know how to let the wind out of your sails when you are about to go into the many reasons and benefits of allowing us to have sodas available in the house. With the lack of bottles lying around our house, I had to search elsewhere.

With wagon in tow, I began my weekly tour of the neighborhood. I went from house to house and asked the owners if they would like for me to dispose of their unwanted bottles that took up valuable space in their homes. Even at seven years old I was quite the con artist when it came to speaking. I would tell them how much cleaner and neater their homes would look without all those unsightly bottles just lying there. I really think my words were bigger than I was because of my love for reading. I would sit and read through the dictionary just to find words I could use that Sherry wouldn't understand. What strange things we do when we are young.

After going from door to door to gather my booty, I would head up the street to Carolinda Road. That street ran from EllisonWilson Road all the way to US 1 and at the end was my destination, The Highway Sundries. This was a little store that was truly one of the original convenience stores. There were no gas pumps to draw the traveler in, only the idea of a cool drink, a snack or maybe just some conversation. It was a gathering place for many workmen after their long day of toiling. They would come and purchase either a cold beer or soda and sit outside on the steps and "shoot the bull" as my dad called it with each other. You could be guaranteed to hear at least one fish story and the promise that the next time, that fish better watch out. There was a comfort in hearing the old timers talk about the past with one another and sharing common beliefs in what they saw of the future. It was a time when people had time for each other and time to just sit and talk. Everyone wasn't in a big hurry to get anywhere but where they were.

I miss those days when time seemed to be our friend instead of the constant enemy that we just don't have enough of it to make everything fit into our day. I don't recall any of the men looking at their watches in a frantic manner worried they were late to some important rendezvous. Most were fathers and husbands stopping for a quick dose of beverage and small talk. These were men on their way home from work and relaxing with friends while they let the trouble of the day pass from them before going home to their honey and children. I don't ever remember my dad bringing his work problems or frustrations of the job into our home. I am not an advocate of going to bars after work to alleviate your stress levels before going home. It just seems a shame there are not places where people can meet if only for ten to fifteen minutes a day to share a laugh or hear a talltale just to let some of the steam off.

That old roadside store was in a time before the 7-ll's and Quik Marts. When the first PDQ came to town and set up business two blocks down the highway with all the convenience of gas and grocery's, it really hurt that little market. There were still the regulars but it wasn't enough to provide the sales needed to stay open. The people that ran the little store weren't just storekeepers, but they were friends to everyone that lived in the area and to many in the communities nearby. I was sad to see the old store close its doors. So many memories of walking through the front doors and seeing Roland or his wife, Papoose (a nickname he gave her and the only name I knew her by) standing behind the counter. My route once inside was to turn left to the comics, candy and ice cream box. Sodas were still in a drink box that opened from the top like a chest freezer and the tops were pried off the bottles not twisted. Between the ice cream and the comics stood a rack of toys filled with everything from bags of army men to coloring books and crayons. There was a smell to the place that the new stores would never have. With their home at the back of the store, you could often smell dinner cooking and it would waif into the front of the building. That little store smelled like home and the people there always welcomed you in with genuine smiles and hospitality.

The money I earned with my bottle venture brought me a lot more than candy and comics. I found a sense of community and family, although extended far beyond my bloodlines, I never the less felt a part of all that was happening. By the time The Highway Sundries closed its' doors I was no longer collecting bottles. The bottling companies did away with deposits on bottles and began pushing can drinks as the most portable. At the end of my bottle business, deposit had gone from two cents on the bottle to five cents. You would have thought I would have been able to buy a lot more, but not so. For as the deposit went up, so did the price of the drink and everything else seemed to follow.

> Ecclesiastes 3:1-8, "To every thing there is a season, and a time to every purpose under heaven: A time to be born, and a time to die; a time to plant, and a time to pluck up that which is planted;

A time to kill, and a time to heal; a time to break down, and a time to build up; A time to weep, and a time to laugh; a time to mourn, and a time to dance; A time to cast away stones, and a time to gather stones together; a time to embrace, and a time to refrain from embracing; A time to get, and a time to lose; a time to keep, and a time to cast away; A time to rend, and a time to sew; a time to keep silence, and a time to speak; A time to love, and a time to hate; a time of war, and a time of peace. "

Not every time is a time I would cherish yet every time is a time to embrace since we are unable to change time. I miss many of the people and places of old that are gone far from me, yet I embrace the memory of each and am glad I had the chance to live in a time of sharing with them. Time cannot be held in a bottle, yet as I think of the hour glass holding the many grains of sand trickling into the bottom half, I can see where we try to capture time inside that glass frame. Time will never be stopped by any of those living or dead, but the day will come when time will cease and eternity will begin; are you ready? I believe that many of the people spoken about in the beginning of this story felt like they had many tomorrows ahead not seeing the day their lives would end. There is no guarantee of tomorrow for any of us, make each moment of each day count.

Burnt Bridge

Where do you start when you have story after story of your darling sister and her fear of crabs? Somewhere in my mind I am sure that she developed this unnatural fear long before I ever came on the scene. You remember she is four years older than I am so it seems only natural that this fear was grounded within her during her formative years, meaning those four years before I was birthed. Since I have no memory before my fourth year, she really had a good eight-year start before I became a menace to her. If you were to ask her where this fear developed she would no doubt point an accusing finger at me. I guess we all need someone to blame for our weaknesses and she blames me.

I will admit to aiding in her torment and possibly continuing the "fear of the CLAW", although I cannot take full responsibility. My dear dad actually was my accomplice, although it was unknown to him. One of my greatest joys was going fishing with Daddy. It did not matter if it was behind the house, on Uncle Jim's dock or wherever there was water to throw in a line. Daddy grew up on that riverbank and in my opinion, knew everything there was about fishing. He taught us how to fish with cane poles equipped with red and white bobbers that attached just above the hook. We would sit for hours and watch those floating sentries waiting for the signal that some giant creature from the deep had taken our bait. Bait that consisted of anything from bacon to bologna or worms that were dug out of the yard, all the way to shrimp that was purchased at the local bait shop.

Daddy had a refrigerator in the garage; we called an "icebox", a term from an era even before my time. It was here that we kept our bait and the prized catch of the day after cleaning them. It was also the box where Daddy kept his beer and if we were lucky to have sodas, they were stashed in there also. Whenever Momma and Daddy were having a get-together that icebox came in handy to keep the extra things that were going to be used for the party. The unfortunate thing about them having a party was Sherry and I would have to clean out the refrigerator of all the stinky things that might have been left in it. This was a time before frost-free freezers and ice usually had developed on all the walls of the little freezer. Ice so thick you had trouble closing the freezer door. Today that would be a real problem with refrigerator/freezer combos having separate doors. This was not the case, for the little freezer was inside the unit at the top with its own little entry door. There were times when you could close the large outer door yet not be able to close the little freezer. It wasn't always a problem to me since I could still fit my box of frozen shrimp in a small space. Momma on the other hand did not see this as a benefit, even though I would try to explain how the extra ice inside helped to keep the things in the refrigerator part really cold. She never fell for that reasoning and made us clean the huge blocks of ice out of the freezer.

The refrigerator had to be unplugged to begin defrosting. Then the door was to be left open so the warm outside air could aid in the melting process. If we waited too late to begin this, then the unit wouldn't have enough time to chill Daddy's beer back to a temperature where it was fit to drink. We made that mistake once and learned that beer needs to be cold to be enjoyed. It made a real impression when Daddy wouldn't drink his normal can of beer after work because it was warm and nasty. I really did not understand why it would be nasty if it was warm since most of what I drank was not really cold and there didn't seem to be a difference. To this day I still prefer a drink with no ice and water to be room temperature. And yes, if I drink sodas today I would prefer one that is cool to the touch but not cold.

Getting back to fishing and the finer things taught; leads me to the rod and reel. My dad was a purist and never used a spinning reel. We were taught how to use the standard open reel and how to hold your thumb on the spool of fishing line while gracefully casting your line into the deep. Graceful is a word I use loosely and you would understand if you were present when we would cast our lines. Anyone that has ever fished with a rod and reel should have a keen awareness of "backlash". The dreaded thing that happens when you don't keep enough pressure on the spool when casting your line. It is the most tangled mess of fishing line ever created. Sometimes it was difficult to determine where the tangle started and where it ended. Sherry was the queen of backlash. She spent more time with her hook either out of the water or in the deep but unable to reel anything in because of the tangled mess in her reel. Daddy never complained about repeatedly untangling her line, in fact I think sometimes I actually saw a slight smile on his face as she would walk to him with her rod and reel in hand. The backlash was always accompanied with a lip that hung down in such a sorrowful pout that you couldn't help but take pity on her and her lack of ability. I think she was more fearful of the possible blister she would get on her thumb if she cast her line with the proper tension, then she was of making Daddy mad with the continual plea for help. Cane poles were for the shallow waters and lazy days. Rods and reels were for days of serious fishing. With a day of serious fishing ahead Daddy loaded his old green panel truck with fishing rods and tackle and then called for Sherry and me to "get a move on" so our adventure could begin. With everything needed for a grand day we headed to a new fishing spot, 703. 703 was the number of the road that led from Juno to Singer Island. Years later it would cross US 1 on the west side of the highway and be known as PGA Boulevard. But this story takes place before PGA was developed in Palm Beach Gardens and before there was a road named after it.

The two-lane 703 was a pleasant road to travel if you were headed for the beach at Singer Island, an island that was part of Riviera Beach. Not the entire island was in Rivera Beach but much of the south end was part of that city. I seem to remember several bridges along 703 that actually connected several smaller islands to the larger ones. This was an area that was always in danger during hurricanes and the evacuation route signs are there to testify to the seriousness of living on an island during storms. It seems so strange to me as I grew older to realize where I grew up was also an island connected by a series of drawbridges. Bridges that were to be closed to the mainland during storms, but that is another story.

The very first bridge once you turned onto 703 was known as "the burnt bridge". A very strange name for a structure made with concrete and steel that showed no signs of fire. Years before the original wooden bridge had burnt and was replaced by its current occupant. Although no remains were left, it was forever known to the locals as "burnt bridge" probably because of the excitement stirred by the event. This was a favorite place to stop and drop in a line because the bridge spanned a small channel that led into a hidden lake where anything from snapper to manatees could be found. Even an occasional shark could be spotted at times depending on the time of year. Then there was also the draw of the 703 restaurant.

Not sure if it ever had a name other then 703, but the little open-air diner was located on the west side of the bridge. It was similar to many of the little eateries built in South Florida at that time. It opened on three sides, this one facing north with the kitchen in the middle of the building and storage at the back. The counter top was visible when the awnings were raised but concealed when closed down. Along all three sides were stools attached to the ground on the outside that stood every type of weather. There were no screens or windows to enclose the diners or prevent insects from entering the establishment. It was a place to sit in the shade and sip on a cool drink or satisfy your raging hunger.

They sold everything from hamburgers and french fries to feed the fisherman, to live minnows and frozen shrimp to feed the fish. The idea of a restaurant/bait shop combination is probably not the health inspectors ideal business coupling, yet I never heard anyone complain to the union. I never cared whether they kept the bait in the same freezer as the ground beef, not that they did, I just did not know. What I did know was Daddy was sure to stop either going or coming back and we would get a soda. By now you should have determined that getting a soda pop was a real treat and not something we had everyday.

If our day was long then sometimes on the way home we would be treated to a hamburger and fries. These were meals that were prepared as you ordered. No pre-made burgers and fries sitting under heat lamps. We would sit and watch as our sandwiches were assembled with layer upon layer of fresh cut tomatoes and lettuce torn right off the head before our eyes. Onions were sliced as needed and whenever onion rings were ordered, they were battered and fried right before our eyes. There was a flavor that was generated long before the product ever crossed your lips as you sat patiently waiting for your food with the smells wafting passed your nostrils as it cooked. Something about eagerly waiting for your food as you saw it getting closer and closer to being finished and put on a plate made our mouths water with anticipation. I am surprised we didn't drool on the counter as we watched.

With everything necessary for a great day of fishing, we set off for a new place to cast in our lines. Daddy choose a spot that had a wonderful opening facing out toward a little grouping of islands known as Munion (rhymes with onion) island. The fact there were very few trees on that side of the road made it even better for our casting. If there were a tree nearby, either Sherry or me would eventually get our line snagged in it. The small seawall became our seat once our lines were in the water. It always appeared that Daddy knew just the right spot where we could not only fish but also a place where we could play. Hard to believe we would sometimes get bored if the fish weren't biting but it did occasionally happen. This place had a nice area off the road where we could run and play. Knowing this road today, you would be putting your lives in peril if you played in the same spot. Once Daddy had the equipment unloaded, we settled in for a day of fishing.

I don't remember any of the fish caught that day. What I do recall is the fun I had with the Blue Crabs that kept taking my bait. Each time I pulled in a crab, the race began. I would swing my fishing rod to whatever side Sherry was sitting and with screams ensuing she would run like a madman. Of course I had to follow with my catch dangling from the end of my line swinging ever closer to her with each step. Daddy would holler for me to stop chasing her and put the crab down, but it was too much fun. I was prepared for the punishment as long as I had the satisfaction of delivering my bounty to Sherry. The problem was when the crab fell off my line; I too would run in horror. I had seen what a crab could do with its claws; I had a vivid memory of a land crab with its claws around our cat's throat choking the life from it. Each time the crab dropped to the ground, Daddy would walk over, pick it up and throw it back into the water. It was just as much fun to watch Sherry when she would catch a crab. The pole was thrown down and she would run, screaming of course. Daddy again coming to the rescue and throwing the crab back to its' home. Although Blue Crabs are very good to eat, we never took any home from our trips. At least not the trips we made to 703.

The memories of days now gone and a place only seen in my mind will still capture my heart with thoughts of laughter and sometimes screams. I sometimes miss the carefree days of youth and wish for the slow pace when spending time together wasn't something you have to schedule into your day. We've gotten into such a hurry with everything that you need an appointment just to spend time with your friends and loved ones. Not everyone has fallen into the trappings of the rush of today, but so many have been caught in its snare. That time spent with Daddy learning the finer art of fishing still ranks as some of the greatest moments in my young life. He never showed a favorite between Sherry and me, and made a point that we understood there would never be one more important than the other.

> *Romans 2:10-12a, "But there will be glory and honor and peace from God for all who obey Him, whether Jews or Gentiles. For God treats everyone the same. He will punish sin wherever it is found." Living Bible*

Daddy was not one to quote the Bible, but he was someone that lived by what it spoke. He was quick to break up trouble between Sherry and me, yet slow to deliver punishment without cause and reason. I often wonder what kind of a child my dad had been to be so tolerant of our shenanigans. I remember the days on 703 and the open-are diner at burnt bridge. I remember the days spent with Sherry and Daddy and my heart is glad.

The Eye of the Storm

Where do you begin with hurricanes when you live in Florida? Whether you have been a resident your entire life or someone that has moved there within the last several years, it is guaranteed you have some knowledge of storms. I was amazed as a child to sit on a dock fishing and watch rain approach along the waterway. To see the evidence of rain, smell the presence of rain, yet it never came to my side of the river. Aunt Clara told me once that was called a sun shower. An occurrence where the sun shines while droplets of rain cascade down. In the middle of a Florida summer it would create an outdoor sauna, especially if you were anywhere near blacktop. The steam would rise like a cloud and on really hot days you could feel it burning your flesh as it made contact with your skin.

I remember days spent at the beach, playing in the surf and then running to move my beach towel and belongings to get out of the path of a waterspout making it way toward shore. Sometimes you could watch the funnel of water for a long time as it would dance and sway on top of the waves never knowing which direction it might be headed. That was the closest I ever came and ever hope to come to anything resembling a tornado. Year's later Sherry and I took Momma back to Minneapolis, Kansas for her

55th high school reunion and stayed in a hotel in Salina. During the night, Momma woke us about 2:00am concerned that we might be having a tornado. The sound was something between a low- pitched whistle and an unearthly moan that made my skin crawl. I called the front desk and asked for an advisory. The clerk was puzzled by my request. I questioned the horrible wind and the fact the window in our room was vibrating, at which time I was informed that was normal. No tornado, just an every night occurrence of strong winds. Kansas, a state where people actually choose to reside. I can't imagine. Although it is very beautiful in the crosscut patterns of farmlands with miles and miles of wheat and com, I just don't think I would want to live there.

I understand every state has things that would not be every person's idea of the perfect place to live. We can choose from hurricanes to tornadoes. Earthquakes, snowstorms or intense heat can be found in various states coupled with volcanoes, mudslides, flooding and every sort of unusual weather pattern available. There may not be the "perfect" state, but every one of the fifty bound together by the United States of America is still the best place in the world. What a diverse land we live in. We have everything from the tropical tips of Texas and Florida on the continental mass, to paradise in the Hawaiian Islands, then back to extreme ice in the arctic areas of Alaska. Deserts to lush forests, mountains, valleys and fields marry together in a union of beauty and splendor. Rivers and streams thread across the land mass joining lakes and oceans. How awesome is this land we share? How awesome is the Creator?

My first encounter with a hurricane was when I was only six years old. In 1960, there were several storms to develop but the first one I recall was Hurricane Donna. It was memorable because it was the first time I ever saw Momma and Daddy preparing for its arrival. Daddy had always told us before that we didn't have to worry about storms because he built our house to withstand the high winds and the pressure associated with hurricanes and tropical storms. But there was something different about this storm. Suddenly they were making preparations for power outages and filling the bathtub with water. Daddy took the old kerosene lantern from the garage and brought it inside. The presence of that old lantern alone made an impact because it was never before allowed to enter the house. It was really dirty and covered with dust from years of hanging outside. The only time it was ever used was for night fishing.

There is an element of fear when you are suddenly thrust into a flurry of activities with preparations for an oncoming storm. Being six years old and already scared of everything did not help although I was reassured over and over again that everything would be all right. Daddy went outside and put large sheets of plywood over all the awning windows. It created an eerie feeling with light now being blocked from the filling each room. The windows on the front porch were jalousies from top to bottom. The small louvered glass panes were many in number to fill the large living room windows. Three windows side by side opened into the living room, with two smaller ones over the sinks in the kitchen. These were not covered with wood. Daddy said the large roof covering the porch should give some protection. Then there were the wall to wall jalousies in the Florida room that faced the Intracoastal Waterway. They were the biggest challenge to cover. Daddy worked long and hard trying to cover all that glass from destruction. Somehow he was able to cover all the windows in that room with the exception of the glass on the doors on either side of the room.

Once our home was secure, Daddy left for Palm Beach. McLaren Construction was under contract with many of the large mansions on the island. It was their duties to board up the windows and make whatever preparations were needed to brace for the storm. Daddy was the foreman at that time and he went with crews to various homes to secure them. It was always a challenge to get everything done before the bridges were closed to the mainland. Most of the homes were vacant during storm season since they usually occurred in the late summer or early fall. Many of the mansions were empty until the "season" began. The "season" started full swing just before Thanksgiving and usually was coming to a close toward the end of April. With Daddy gone to Palm Beach, we waited with Momma as the rain began to fall. I did not understand why so much was being done to prepare for this storm. Why was it so different from the others? I watched as Momma checked and double- checked the supplies. We had a box of candles, numerous books of matches, one oil lamp that had never been out of the kitchen cabinet (at least in my short lifetime) and then there was that old fishing lantern. I remember the oil lamp vividly. It was one of those things that was a, "I can't reach it, but I can see it, and I'm not allowed to touch it". Anyone that was a child, which includes you, knows exactly what that meant. If it was not to be touched, something inside compelled you to find a way to see it up close. The only thing that saved me was the fact that it sat on the highest shelf in the kitchen and I knew it would take time to get there, so much time to the point I would be caught. When you have so many things that are "don't do, and can do" suddenly crossing lines that were before taboo; it makes quite an impact.

While there were many of our neighbors that had animals living outside that would need to be secured in a safe area, we only had a housedog and cat. The dog was a black and tan Manchester, not sure what that really is, but she was very small and very round named Kenna. Momma said she was in the Chihuahua family but she did not look like the dog that was later used for Taco Bell as their national spokes dog. She did have the same shape head but that ends the similarities. Kenna was Mom's dog and was usually wherever Momma was. In the hustle to prepare for the on coming storm, Kenna was unusually bound to Mom's ankles and was determined to not let her out of sight. The cat, known as "Fat face", his real name was Mack, was far too busy watching the hustle and bustle to get involved. He watched from whatever perch he chose at that time and seemed bothered if he was in any way disturbed. It was not until the peak of the storm that he demonstrated any uneasiness. Even then it was only to move to a place with everyone else so he was assured there was safety.

After all preparations were made Momma began to call others as Hurricane Donna approached land. Calls to Grandma and Grandpa were somewhat calming to Momma as she heard that they were prepared to face the storm. She called everyone in the family to verify they were okay. But the person she called the most was Aunt Beebe. Aunt Beebe was Dad's twin sister and she lived in West Palm Beach. She was married to Uncle Frankie who worked with Daddy. The frequent calls were to see if Uncle Frankie was home yet, because if he was home it meant that Daddy would be home soon. When they left Palm Beach, Daddy would drop Uncle Frank off as he passed through West Palm on his way home. Many of the phone calls I think were also a chance to feel connected to others rather than being isolated. Even though Sherry and I were with Momma while we waited, there had to be a feeling of emptiness without Daddy there to be our anchor. His steady calm nature was a blessing so many times when it seemed the world was troubled and uncertain. Once Daddy arrived home it became a waiting game. This was a time before cell phones and portable telephones. The newest thing to happen to our telephone was to lose the name before the number. Our number started with Victor 4, which became VI4 and then the last four digits completed the number. We still had rotary dial telephones and watched television via antenna that had to be lowered in anticipation of high winds. With the antenna lowered we had very little channels to watch and stayed glued to whatever news we could get as the storm approached.

It was almost surreal as we sat in the house, gathered together in the living room where it would usually be light and sunny at that time of day. Yet now it was eerie and dark with not only the windows blocking light, but nothing coming through the darkened skies. As we waited there was an uneasiness that could be felt. An uncertainty permeated the air and seemed to cover us like a cloak. Daddy had been through several "killer storms" in his lifetime and knew what could happen if you took things for granted. He had been through the storm with no name in 1928, that killed so many that there still has not been an accurate number available for the records. He told us later of the government digging huge holes and burying bodies in massive graves. The death toll was numbered mostly be the "white" people that were lost. You need to remember that was a time before equality was available for African-Americans. Daddy said there were hundreds of migrant workers maybe thousands of blacks and Hispanics that were dead, many unaccounted for, as their bodies were never found. I know there are still barriers of prejudice in this country, but I thank God for the progress that has been made. I just pray that we never fall back and will always move forward toward a nation of love and brotherhood of every race and every color.

In 1928, Daddy was eleven years old when that killer storm arrived. Pop and Mom McLaren lost all their livestock but no human lives. As soon as it was safe to go out they went to check their land. Finding the turkeys and pigs dead, yet still fresh, they hung them up to bleed and butchered the meat to eat. The meat was then given to many of their neighbors who had no food and no means to get any with the roads blocked. The fresh turkey and pork was able to sustain many, including my Dad and his family until they were able to get to the mainland, or until new stock could be brought over the river. There wasn't a family in Palm Beach County that was not somehow touched by the devastation. The *Weather Channel* has aired Storm Stories about the *"Forgotten Storm"* and it gives many details Daddy did not know Then there was the old bridge down near Pop's that was a constant reminder of what a hurricane could do. The only part left standing after a storm in 1949 was the concrete portion that housed the gears to raise the draw span. It was at the end of McLaren Road and a favorite place to fish. The bridge was left open so large boats could go through to safety in the waterway, but the winds tore the draw spans from their base and crumpled the concrete on the western side of the river. Leaving a lone reminder of what once had been, but would never be again. The bridge was never rebuilt with the construction of a new bigger, stronger bridge spanning the waterway on US 1 only a quarter of a mile down river.

As we waited for Donna the winds began to grow stronger and the rain came in sheets. When it appeared that our angry visitor had arrived, Daddy moved us all into their master bedroom on the north side of the house. There we had no light at all except the lamps on the nightstand and dresser while we still had power. The fact there was a bathroom connected to their bedroom was a real plus. Now with the windows covered and all doors closed, it appeared smaller than normal being filled with the dog the cat and us. There were supplies of candles and boxes of matches lying next to a flashlight on the dresser. On the chest of drawers sat the once forbidden oil lamp. With electricity still available we sat together watching the TV and trying to pickup channel 4 out of Miami. They had some of the best hurricane tracking at that time.

Sometime in the wait, I fell asleep. Even with all the fears that I fought as a child, in the midst of the storm I felt safe. When I awoke it was to lamp light and the sound of the small transistor radio giving updates on the storm. It seemed that Donna had passed with the main force bearing south of Palm Beach County. Still, we had lost power and the winds were in a continuous moan. As I looked around the room, I saw Sherry asleep on the floor next to me and Momma was in bed. With the windows blocked, I could not tell if it were day or night. Daddy slept on the other side of Momma and while lying on the floor I was unable to see if he was there. I was scared to move too much thinking I might disturb Sherry's sleep and then she would be mad.

As I lay listening to the rain, I noticed that the wind had lessened and the raindrops were not as hard. I was such an inquisitive child; I had questions running wild in my mind. What time was it? How long had I been asleep? Should I wake someone up and let them know that I was awake? Was it okay to get up and go to the bathroom or should I wait? Was Daddy awake? Where was the dog and cat? Who lit the oil lamp? How long had we been without power? Why was I the only one awake?

Just as I was about to get into trouble by getting up and probably stepping on Sherry during my trek to the bathroom, the bedroom door opened. There was a small amount of light coming in from the dining room and the silhouette of someone coming into the room. Not seeing who it was I jumped to my feet and hollered, "Someone's here!" That quickly shook everyone from sleep. With everyone now awake, Daddy stepped into the room and looked around at his family with a smile and said, "The storm has passed and we are fine." Those words settled my fears knowing everything was okay. Although my idea of fine and Daddy's were different, we did come through the storm without loss of life. We did lose power for several days and lived like campers, only indoors.

There was much to be done outside. Not only the uncovering of the windows, but now there was also the clean up of the yard and driveway. We couldn't have left the house even if the roads were cleared because of the huge Oak limbs that had come down in the storm. There were branches and tree limbs down all over the neighborhood. Power lines and poles were either broken or the transformers had blown limiting power to many homes and businesses. The next few days of cleanup were to enable us to safely move around the yard. We were fortunate, as our home was not damaged in any way. There were many that lost roofs and had trees fall on their homes crushing walls and breaking windows. It still amazes me the amount of stress the trees can handle without blowing over. The roots of the Live Oaks grow very deep, according to Daddy and he said that God made the Palm trees to bend and sway with the wind. Sitting on the patio during one of his breaks at cleanup, Daddy explained how man has learned to build structures to withstand hurricanes by watching trees and nature. He told how God designed the Earth to survive and there is no greater architect. At six I didn't know what an architect was but I knew it was someone smart, or they could never understand the things of God.

Before leaving Florida in 1983, I had experienced many storms. There were a few that stay in my mind. In 1964, there were several storms late in the summer. I am not sure if it was Cleo or Isabell that passed right over our home with the eye. I do remember going out into the eye of the storm. It was an experience I have never forgotten. There is something so unnatural when you hear wind howl for hours and suddenly, silence. Daddy looked over at me and said, "Come on, let's check to see if everything is secure". When we stepped out the door onto the front porch there was an eerie quiet. No wind, no birds, no sound but us. Several of our patio chairs had blown into the hedge and Daddy called for me to come help him gather them into the garage. As we were walking back to the house we spotted an awesome sight. Hours before we had chained our ski boat to the Springfield Mango tree and filled it with water. The trailer and motor were stored safely in the garage but there wasn't enough room to leave the boat on the trailer. To keep it from blowing away, the plug that would normally take water out of the boat was put in place to now keep water in. The boat still full of water was moved to the other side of the tree, still chained with no visible signs of the move. What an awesome sight!

One of the storms in the 60's brought the water table high enough to reach our back door. When you live only three feet above sea level, it doesn't take a huge surge to raise the water. To give you a better understanding of why that is significant, I should tell you that our backdoor was at least seventy-five feet from the seawall. The water had to rise enough to come over the seawall and still swell to reach the foundation of our Florida room. I remember standing inside the backdoor with Sherry and feeling the excitement as we saw little waves break against the back walls of the house. That was the year that the *Honey-Fitz*, a yacht owned by the Kennedy's was anchored behind our seawall. I recall Daddy joking about whether the water would raise enough until their boat was docked against our house.

If you were to look at all the storms that have come and gone during the years I lived in Florida, you would find enough to fill a journal. It amazes me when I look at the history of hurricanes and tropical storms that came every year during my youth. I don't recall all of them only a select few. What I do recall is the calm assurance Daddy radiated in the midst of chaos.

> *Isaiah 43:2-Ja, "When you pass through the waters, I will be with you; and through the rivers, they will not overflow you: when you walk through the fire, you will not be burned; neither will the flame be kindled upon you. For I am the Lord your God, the Holy one of Israel, your Savior:"*

Each storm brought a sense of urgency to prepare as it drew near. The steps varied very little through the years. The only thing that had changed was the aluminum awnings Momma and Daddy had installed on the house after Hurricane Donna. The awnings were light enough and simple to handle so that Sherry and I were able to cover the windows giving Daddy more time to get things done in Palm Beach, and then to come home sooner. Each of us had a responsibility to prepare for the arrival of the hurricane.

In later years there were many people that began to have "hurricane parties" and wait for the storm to come while they drank and joked about the impending doom. There have been times where some while still in their party manner, were caught unaware by the winds and have died. Daddy said that people that have no respect for the unpredictability of nature are like someone trying to dance with a twister. There would never be a question as to who would lead in that dance. Even some of the lesser hurricanes have caused much damage and even loss of life.

Life is a precious gift. A gift given by a Father that has only the greatest aspirations for us. A Father that loves us more than any can imagine. And although we sometimes will speak or sing of the greatness of God's love, still our minds grasp only a small peek of how much that really might be. Whether we go through the storm or the fire, He is with us and will always take care of us. Just as I could sense a calm in the midst of chaos because of the calm that Daddy displayed before us, so too should we rest in the calm of our Father's love.

I once asked Daddy when I had grown into my teens if he was ever afraid during the storms. He told me that he was scared with each storm not knowing what it would bring, but he also knew that he could either show fear or peace for us to see. He knew that we were scared enough and needed someone to be strong. In the midst of his fears he learned to lean on God to take us through. I too have learned this one simple thing in life. We actually have only two choices for every situation: Trust God or don't trust God. It is really that simple. So as the storms of life come your way, learn to trust in the Father and know that he will bring calm in the midst of chaos.

Summers on the Farm

Growing up I had a wonderful friend named Becky. She was the granddaughter of a lady named Gena Strode who was my grandma's best friend. We all went to church together at the Christian Training Centre in West Palm Beach, where my grandparents were the pastors. Becky was a little older than me with her birthday being in June and mine in July. We both lived in what was at that time, the rural parts of Palm Beach County. I lived just outside North Palm Beach and she lived just outside Jupiter. Jupiter was farther north and even more unpopulated than where I lived. It was in fact, the last city to pass through before you left Palm Beach County on the north end and entered into Martin County.

West of Jupiter where Becky lived was a place where people bought acres of land and not lots. It was filled with miles of small and big farms where the natural landscape was left except for places to either grow crops or graze animals. You could drive for miles on dirt roads that gave the appearance that you were headed no where, then suddenly there would be a house. Most of the time it might seem you were lost, especially if you had no directions to your destination and God forbid if you had taken a wrong tum. You could drive for miles without spotting someone to ask information. The fortunate thing was because there were so few homes; everyone seemed to know who and where each of the other occupants lived.

When summer approached, Sherry and I knew we would be able to spend some of it with Becky and her brother Bo at their farm. It was not a huge place maybe consisting of less than one hundred acres, but there was enough land and places to explore for us to stay busy. Gena and Jim Strode were Becky's grandparents and they lived in the big white farmhouse that was at the end of drive. Becky was always there so it was years before I realized that she and her family lived in the house next door. The farmhouse had a large screened in porch that formed an "L" wrapping around the right side of the house with chairs and sofas for relaxing. There were numerous small tables and a screened door on the front and one on the side both with long springs to close them when going either in or out. When we were visiting there was a continual slam with each opening and someone to holler, "Stop slamming the door".

The kitchen was large enough to fit several people at one time yet small enough to still have a cozy feeling. The smell of fresh biscuits baking was one of my favorite memories. When they were in the oven it seemed the aroma would waif out the doors and windows and find you wherever you were. Unless we were far away, those biscuits would hunt us down. I don't know if it is true, but I always thought that something was cooking all the time. Every time we entered the house, it was through the kitchen and into the living room, so to think that something was cooking all the time; it really might have been with the smell of cooking continually filling the air.

To the west end of the living room was a small stairwell that led to a sleeping space that was part of the attic that they had finished and decorated. It too was comfy and cozy and often a place to rest. Strange but true, I don't really recall where we slept, just the days leading up to the utter exhaustion causing us to fall immediately into a deep sound sleep. The days were long hot and filled with much to do. And everyday started with those piping hot biscuits with jam, jelly or honey. Sometimes there was molasses and sorghum to choose from making the decision that much harder.

The house was surrounded by a yard wrapped with a fence to separate it from the pastures and the barnyard. In the front yard, next to the gate was a small platform with steps leading to the top that was used for mounting horses for those too small to reach a stir-up from the ground.

That included most of us when we were really little. As we grew older, there wasn't always the need for assistance, unless you were going to ride one of Jim's horses. He had two horses that were always nearby, one brown and one white. The brown horse was named Ginger and the white one, Skipper. Both were very tall which was odd to me with Jim being a small man. I later learned that Jim had once been a jockey, which was understandable with his small stature. Although he was small, he had no fear of horses and those two giants he rode obeyed his direction.

Becky had a palomino Quarter Horse named Bobby Socks that she called Bobby for short. Bobby was a beautiful horse with a golden body and flaxen colored mane and tail. Each leg was white from the hoof up to about six to eight inches above, and thus the name Bobby Socks. Bobby was usually the horse Becky rode when we went on our little adventures around the farm. Sherry rode one of the other horses, but I don't recall which one. I was always given Billy. Billy was a pony that had to be caught before we could ride. It would sometimes take us thirty minutes or more to catch Billy with him as determined to avoid us and we were determined to catch him. It was always a battle of wits to see which of us could coach him into a smaller pen where he could be cornered tied and eventually saddled. This was always against his will and he was never lax in showing his disapproval.

Where in our thinking did we miss the fact that Billy really did hate to be saddled and rode? Each time I would reach my foot toward the stir-up he would immediately begin to move. Sometimes just a step or two forward and other times he went in circles, each time with me hopping along side trying to mount. If it hadn't been such work to get on him it probably would have been funny. I recall Sherry laughing several times making me mad and frustrated. Although I do have to admit, if it had been someone else other than me, I too would have chuckled.

After many struggles, I finally was seated atop a completely unwilling ride. As we started off for a day of adventure, I tried to settle both Billy's attitude and mine. I remember gently speaking to him trying to soothe his anger. I tried softly stroking his neck and reassuring him that it really was okay. No matter what I tried it was all to no avail. He was determined to end this union as quickly as possible. One event in particular I remember was the day we were nearing the bridge to take us over the creek that separated the farm from the road. These creeks were manmade by the Department of Engineering and the Road Department to help with flood control. They were approximately four to six feet deep and in some places up to twelve feet wide. Without rain there would be very little water in those ditches, but when it rained the water would rush just like a flowing river. It was during this time when there was an abundance of water still in the ditches that Billy and I created one lasting memory.

We were riding toward the bridge with full intention of crossing to the open road and then across to the land where they kept many of their cattle. When we were within a hundred yards of the opening, Billy took off in a full run heading toward the creek. With me screaming WHOA and pulling back on the reins as hard as I could he continued with determination that he would reach that creek. The truth is… he never made it completely there, but I did. Just as he came to the edge he came to a complete and abrupt stop. He stopped but I didn't. With the reins still in my hands, I sailed right over his head and into the water. I don't know if horses can laugh but I swear that he had a look on his face that had the appearance of complete satisfaction and an almost sneer. This was not the only time I had seen that look from that cantankerous brown pony and it definitely would not be the last time.

Billy threw me into that creek, over a fence, into a tree and into a Scrub Palm. Every time but one, I had to again chase him down, either by myself or sometimes with the aid of Bo. The one and last time he pitched me off his back, he ran as fast as he could back to the barn and in a little while, Jim appeared with Skipper to bring me home. After landing in the low hanging branches of a pine tree I was covered with scratches and a few small cuts. With my body already in pain, it took quite a bit from both Jim and me to get me up on the high back of that huge horse. Even though we were a distance from the farm, still Jim lead Skipper back to the barn with me in saddle. I never knew why he didn't mount and ride with me since there was plenty of room on Skipper's long back. But he walked slow and easy leading that goliath with me aboard and as he led I could feel the aches easing in my body. That was the last year I was to ride Billy, thank God! But that was not the end of our adventures. I was later given a horse, not a pony, but a real horse to ride and although it must have been good, I don't seem to have the memories that have stuck with me from my rides with Billy. I guess it is true that we tend to remember the bad things in life more than the good, especially with the bad making such an impression.

There were hot summer days when we would go down to the small pond and spend the afternoon fishing. It was not a pond for swimming, at least for me, since it was full of snapping turtles and sometimes a snake or two. I have never enjoyed the idea of swimming with something that could bite off my fingers and toes or that could kill me. Growing up around salt water is different from fresh water ponds and rivers. You have a completely different array of reptiles and animals. The many fears that I faced were always bigger when it was something I didn't understand. Saltwater turtles are big and non- aggressive. Freshwater turtles can be non-aggressive until you hear of the "snapping turtle". Someone, probably Sherry told me they would chase you if you got too close to their homes and they could bite of my entire foot. Even though I was not sure if it was true, I still made every effort to avoid them. Years later I saw a large Alligator Snapping Turtle out of the water and someone took a stick to move him out of the way and the turtle snapped that rather stout stick like it was a small twig. I still avoid them.

On our way to the pond or more often on our way back, we would have one of the most unusual fights in the history of farm life, the cow patty fight. This was an event that consisted of dried cow patties found in the field that had been there long enough to form a crust on the outside. When a cow patty dries it becomes light in weight and somewhat crunchy. If your target is too far away you cannot hurl the patty hard enough to strike them. In that case you look for a patty that has formed a crust on the outside to shield your hands from being soiled, yet because of its weight you know it is still moist on the inside. This makes a great weapon to reach the distance the dried out patty could never make. The only problem with the heavier patty is that on impact it burst apart and the moist contents cover your target. This makes for a very ugly fight. I must admit that although those were the worst fights imaginable, they were also the most fun. I will always have memories of walking to the house with small bits of manure covering most of our anatomy and clothing with smiles and laughter that still rings in my ears.

There is still the memory of the day I went into the chicken coop to find eggs and someone, again probably Sherry, turned the latch on the door and I was stuck in there with all those hens. I really didn't mind until the rooster made his entrance through the small hatch door made only big enough for them to go in and out and me with no way of escape. He did not like my presence in that small coop. I wasn't too happy with the accommodations at that moment either. It really turned into a free-for-all when I began to scream and holler. I would yell and he would crow. This went on for what seemed a very long time, although it might have been only seconds, until Bo came and offered to let me out. He didn't just open the door, no he had to stand outside, laughing and asking if I really wanted to come out. What kind of a maniac would have thought I wanted to stay in there? When I was released, I ran as fast as I could away from that bellowing rooster. I still am not overly fond of roosters. To this day, I still have no knowledge as to who it was that turned that latch.

I will never forget summer days of laying in the loft and dreaming dreams of tomorrow with friends I thought would always be a constant in my life. Although Becky and I have not seen each other for years, I will always hold her in my heart and keep her in my prayers. The last time I saw her was at the old place where she was training horses and I think she was giving riding lessons. Some of the old farm had been sold and she was able to keep the barn and had even built a new stable, but it was a sad thing to see the area was developing into a housing division. The dirt roads have all been paved and city water has been run to most of the houses. Land that had been swampy during the rainy season had been filled in and sold at unbelievable prices. I didn't ride over to see if the population expansion had devoured Burt Reynolds ranch, which at one time was sort of next door, remembering that neighbors were many acres apart. I was curious but not enough to drive there to see the changes.

> *Proverbs 18:24, "A man that hath friends must show himself friendly; and there is a friend that sticketh closer than a brother." Proverbs 17:17, "A friend loveth at all times, and a brother (or sister) is born for adversity."*

I was fortunate to have people in my life like Becky and her family. They were so much a part of my youth.

There were many people in my younger days that were not pleasant memories, but I believe it is not healthy to dwell on thoughts that breed hurt and resentment. Wounds often cause pain and leave scars but that should not be the reason to continually point to the scar and remember the hurt. Thank God we can move forward pass all the yesterdays that wounded us. Jesus told us to look ahead and not turn back (Luke 9:62).

> *Paul in Philippians 3:13-14, "No, dear brothers, I am still not all I should be but I am bringing all my energies to bear on this one thing: Forgetting the past and looking forward to what lies ahead, I strain to reach the end of the race and receive the prize for which God is calling us up to heaven because of what Christ Jesus did for us." (LB)*

The past is passed and needs to be left behind where is was and not where we try make it current if there is no good thing to be found. Hold fast to the pleasant memories just as the fragrance of the rose clings to the petals, we too need to let sweetness surround our countenance. To Becky, wherever you are, I miss you my friend and cherish your moments in my life. God bless and keep you always in His care.

Sailing Ships

Sometimes life has a way of laying pieces before us similar to the playing spaces on a board game.

We don't always see the importance of the moment or understand the reasoning behind what we face, but I am convinced of this one thing; all things happen for a reason. There isn't anything in this life that just happens. We strive to make our today better than our yesterday's so that our tomorrow will be the best yet. But what if tomorrow never comes? I see parents working two jobs to provide a living for their children yet fail to teach them how to live. Every generation tries to make life easier for their offspring and give them all the things they, as children, never had. When is enough, enough?

I grew up in the late fifties and sixties when the voice of America was changing. Big Band sounds and classical music was being replaced with a new sound, rock and roll. There was much controversy over the wild beat and the need to turn up the volume until you could feel it in the floor. The ultimate level was when you couldn't distinguish the beat of the song from the beat of your heart. Thump, thump, thump was sound you craved and that was the beginning of the sub-woofer for every teen. People think it has only been the last ten years that music lovers were filling their cars with speakers to achieve the greatest degree of pounding rhythms. It has been evolving with the development of the radio in cars and will continue throughout time.

I have watched as our society has provided our youth with so much that they often have very little incentive to achieve anything on their own. We have given and given until they have learned to stand before us with hand outstretched demanding more. If they get a video system, they need either more games then they will ever really enjoy playing or they need a newer upgraded system like little Tommy next door. We may not be keeping up with the Jones but our kids are keeping up with Tommy.

Then the day comes when they get a car. Not one they've worked to gain, but one that mommy and daddy have saved for to be sure they drive a better, newer car then either of them drives. After all, we don't want someone at school thinking that we can't provide for our children. Not everyone is caught up in the vicious circle of competitive childcare but all of us are guilty of wanting to make things easier than we had it. There is nothing wrong with that desire as long as we are not so determined to provide that we fail in teaching our children how to succeed. Success is not having things in life or how much the bottom line is on your paycheck. Success is to know that if you were gone tomorrow that the future generations would know how to survive. Not to survive with just scraping by or stepping over others, but learning to survive victoriously with peace and contentment.

We need to help our future by allowing kids to dream again. With nurturing their minds and imaginations to reach beyond the small window each of us see through. In making it so much easier we have created many young people that don't know how to work. They weren't taught to be strong in the face of adversity. As an employer I see so many teenagers starting with me as their first job. I want each one to have a great experience but it doesn't always happen. I do know that a first job can either help that young person to learn that they can do what is needed no matter the task, or it can emotionally cripple them with the idea they are useless. It has been difficult to make every new worker feel they had value. Some come already defeated by the words they received at home or school. Then there are the ones I have hired that implied by their actions that they were too good to be doing such menial labor.

Unless they are involved in a team function many children don't know what teamwork is all about. They don't grasp the word commitment and integrity. They may not see that there is anything bigger than their world and their needs. It really isn't all about just you or just me. My parents made us follow through on whatever we committed to as youths. It didn't matter if we were tired or sick, we had to be where we were supposed to be whether it was school, work or church activities. Unless we were "in the bed sick" we were going to be there. That has followed me my entire life, once I was out of high school. School was a different story, but not one to tell now. Back to the caliber of today's new generation, I have been faced with employees calling in sick with allergies while I was working with bronchitis. Too sick to work but not too sick to play basketball with friends. How do we turn the tide?

Tide... That word brings me back to the river's edge where I spent many hours dreaming dreams of a world I would never really embrace, at least not in the natural world. But embrace it I did with my heart and my imagination. James Dobson's *Focus on the Family*, has developed many tools to help develop healthy imaginations in children and one of my favorites is, *Adventures in Odyssey*. At Whit's Comer, Mr. Whittaker has invented an "imagination station" that can send you anywhere. I had my own imagination station in our own backyard.

Sometime before I was born there were two very tall Australian pine trees that stood on the banks of the Intracoastal Waterway on the land where Pop lived. It was actually on the piece of undeveloped property that was between our house and Pop's. I could be mistaken about the type of pine tree, but that was the only name I had ever heard them called. They were very tall stately evergreen trees that grew to be about sixty feet in height and reminded me of giant Christmas trees. The one in our backyard was nearly four feet in diameter at the base and leaned slightly toward the water. It was one of my favorite places to sit and hide when I was in trouble or just when I wanted to have down time. I spent many hours propped against that old tree counting stars at night or looking for cloud shapes in the day.

The two trees that had once stood along the riverbank behind Pop's had fallen prey to the continual dredging that the Corp. of Engineers were doing to aid in widening the river and increasing it's depth. Where at one time my Dad tells me of how he and his family could actually walk across one section of the "canal" during low tide with the width close to thirty feet. The dredging had eaten away the shoreline until the area that had only been thirty feet across was now close to one hundred and fifty feet wide and nearly thirty feet deep. With all the movement of the shoreline, the once stately pines were now fallen reminders of what once had been, but was no more. When they fell into the river, they fell in such a way that their trunks crisscrossed over one another. The trees lay parallel with the bank and were not a threat to on coming ships so they were left to decay naturally.

By the time I discovered the now fallen sentries, their bark had been completely removed by the continuous ravage of the water and waves. What remained of the tree trunks was smooth to touch and gray in color. The gnarled roots of each tree lay at opposite ends with the trunk crossing over each other just above the root line. If you can imagine a spool of thread or yarn, then you can somewhat see how they appeared with a small spindle type area and the larger ends of the spool extending from the water. This was my imagination station for many years. Even before I could swim, I found ways to get to those tree trunks where I became the greatest sea captain of all time. Not only because I was the first female sea captain of a fine galleon, but because I was also the youngest. The base of the one tree had so many gnarled roots there was actually a place for me to sit and be really comfortable. At one side of my captains chair was the long arm of the rudder. That was the end toward the south yet as I sat in the rear of my vessel, I faced north and into the winds. The base on the north or front of my ship was filled with many twisted and overlapping roots that became my controls to operate the necessary levers to raise and lower the great sails. It was in that group of roots that I found a wonderful large root that had somehow circled around the bottom and became the great wheel for steering during rough waters.

At an early age I learned of the high and low tides, not by someone sitting with instruction but because of my connection to the sea. As I would make my way to my ship it was generally at low tide. This made it easy access for boarding with only a small amount of water still under her great hull. I could then play for hours before the tide would become so high that I would have to jump ship and make for shore. You may be wondering where Sherry was, or where my parents were while I was alone on the riverbank for hours. I can honestly tell you, I don't have any idea. I was so determined to reach my great vessel that I probably had tunnel vision only seeing one thing. Momma and Daddy never seemed overly concerned that I would be in trouble or that something bad would happen. With so many neighbors and family nearby, I really think they knew someone would always be watching even if it were someone across the river.

Back to the high sea adventures. I had read *Treasure Island* and seen movies like *2000 Leagues under the Sea. Mutiny on the Bounty* and various movies with swashbucklers and pirates. John Payne and Errol Flynn were always hero's even if they started out on the wrong side, they inevitably turned good. These were the shows and books that made me yearn for high seas and adventure. I had a sword that I carried with me each time I was to embark for another voyage. It was no more than a stick I had found in the wooded area around Pop's house and I knew he wouldn't care if I keep it.

I never had shoes on my feet as I left for the beach. What am I saying, I rarely had shoes on except to go to church or school. But shoes would have been cumbersome aboard ship. I loved the way that sand felt under my feet as I made my way through the shallow water to climb aboard. Then there was the wonderful smooth surface of that old wood. No teakwood deck could have felt any better. The years of waves breaking against them had cleaned every bit of bark and left them with a polished appearance. Yet even as the tide rose and began to cover the top of the trunks, the surface never became slick or slimy.

With the tide always changing, there was a constant flow in the water. While the tide was coming in, the water flowed to the north and when the tide was going out, or low tide; the water flowed to the south. There was never a time that the water sat completely still. With constant movement there was continual change. The most exciting times were when I had to prepare for the oncoming storm. As on any great sea the weather can change in a moment's notice. All great sea captains are prepared for the sudden changes. I would watch the sky to determine if there would be a sudden squall. Often there would be high waves with large swells that my vessel would encounter.

As the weather would turn it became a race to get the sails lowered and the great wheel engaged to steer the ship clear of danger. Even when the sky looked clear, there would be under currents that would cause the waves to beat against her hull. Then there were the unexpected surges in the waves that would try to over turn my craft. Each passing boat created these surges of water. Their direction would determine the flow of the oncoming waves. When the tide was low there wasn't as much to prepare for as the waves slapped against the bottom. But when the tide had risen to a point where the water was already midway up the sides of my ship, then the sudden swells could be quite challenging.

As the tide became high, it also seemed to cause those old stumps to sway in the water with every movement of the current. The trunks were too heavy to float away and they had probably become waterlogged from the many years they laid slumbering along the shoreline, although I have no proof of that fact. The roots that were buried in the sand also appeared to anchor their massive remnants to that spot. Even with the tremendous weight they still had, the movement of the water at high tide was enough to make even the most seaworthy captain a little unsteady on their feet. As the ship would rock back and forth with each new wave I would try to balance myself. I would try to stay afloat as long as possible, but with not knowing how to swim, as the water rose with the tide, I had to jump ship and head toward shore and the safety of dry land.

I had been through hurricane Donna by the time I found this abandoned vessel. So often the storms I would see approaching were hurricanes with names only I knew. One day when a tugboat came through pushing two very large barges that had been secured together; I named that series of waves hammering my ship, hurricane Sherry. I never told her that I named a hurricane after her because I was never sure if she would be honored or if she would pound me. I think that happen just after one of our many fights as siblings and I thought it appropriate to call the next storm after her. If the tide was high each new storm was a hurricane. If the tide was low each storm was a thunderstorm and sometimes a welcome change in the everyday calm.

I sailed on my ship for many years even after I had learned to swim. It had become a place of quiet and peace. A place of familiarity where I was queen of my domain and had to answer to no one. It was where I liked to go when I just wanted to daydream or sometimes I would take my fishing pole and fish from her deck. The water below the hull was clear enough that I could see fish, especially Puffer fish and Grunt, as they would play between the roots. Some areas of the river were dusky and unclear but where we lived the water was clean and the sand was grayish white and reflected to reveal the creatures below.

One day, years later as I was swimming behind our house, my Dad came down to tell me that it was near supper. As he approached the seawall I had heard him coming and began to slowly swim toward shore. When he reached the top of the seawall he motioned for me to stop. I questioned him as to why and he just looked a bit concerned about something so to not upset him any further, I stopped swimming. He told me to stand where I was and with the water only about three feet deep at that point, I stood. Still looking at Dad, he told me to walk very slowly to the beach and to not make much motion. It made me a little nervous the way he was acting but I trusted him and made my way to the seawall. Thoughts of some huge killer shark were lurking in my mind, or possibly a monster stingray. It could be a giant moray eel just looking for lunch and I was available. When I reached the bank, I turned to look at the water and saw that I had been in the middle of a large school of barracuda.

I have been back to Florida and have looked off the seawall behind the old house where I grew up. The seawall is new and the new owners had put in a dock, the one we had spoken of for years but never followed through on the action. But the changes in the water were what tore at my heart. No longer could you see the once flourishing puffer fish, as they have become less in population. The water has become brackish and trash seemed to cling to the shoreline or float along with the tide. Even the smell of the salt in the air had somehow changed. At first I thought maybe it was just along the river where the changes had occurred but when I went to the ocean, it too had an unusual smell and the once inviting mist of salt in the air seemed tainted by pollution.

I am glad and feel very privileged to have grown up in the wonderful state known as the "Sunshine State". Florida was and is still a place of beauty. Although many things have changed and the population has grown considerably since I was small, there is still so much of my heart in the wooded areas along the Intracoastal Waterway. I may have learned much in the time I spent alone, but I learned even more from the heart of a man that I called Daddy.

It has been years now since Daddy has gone to be with the Lord and there isn't a day go by that something doesn't happen to remind me somehow of the man that had become my mentor and my best friend. I can only pray that even though I don't have children of my own, that I can still be an example to others to always know there is a Father out there that cares about them. My Dad and I did not always see eye to eye and there were times that I didn't even like him, but I never stopped loving him. He taught me that things do change in life, just as the tide comes in and goes out. With each change there are new things to float your way and often many things that can float away. Choose what to hold on to and what to let go of with the change of each new direction of the water. And just as it does in the river, if you let something float away from you with one tide, there is a good chance when the tide changes that whatever you let go is going to come floating right pass you again. Learn to let it pass and move on. The only thing to hold tight is love.

> *1 Car. 13:4-8a, "Love endures long and is patient and kind, love never is envious nor boils over with jealousy, is not boastful or*

proud, and does not display itself haughtily. it is not conceited and does not act unbecoming. Love does not insist on its own rights or its own way for it is not self-seeking; it is not touchy or fretful or resentful: it takes no account of the evil done to it. It does not rejoice at injustice and unrighteousness, but rejoices when right and truth prevail. Love bears up under anything and everything that comes, is ever ready to believe the best of every person, its hopes are fadeless under all circumstances, and it endures everything. Love never fails (never fades out or becomes obsolete or comes to and end)"...

Of all the stories I've shared and all the people you have become aquatinted with through the telling of my tales, I hope that you have smiled a time or two and maybe even had an adventure in your life that one of these stories have reminded you of. There are too many tales to tell and I could go on forever, so with that in mind, I will bring this chapter of my young life to a close. I have many more stories to tell and I have enjoyed walking down this trail of memories with you. My one desire is that you too can hear the gentle sounds at the river's edge and maybe one day soon we will travel back one more time to a place of adventures and laughter. Until then, God bless you and keep you in all your ways and learn to love the Words of your Father.

www.ingramcontent.com/pod-product-compliance
Lightning Source LLC
LaVergne TN
LVHW011942070526
838202LV00054B/4767